Much as she loves Maury, Connie realizes their relationship doesn't have a future as long as he fears commitment.

"I'm afraid because I can't give up flying, Connie. And any commitment I could make would require that. I don't think I can live without being able to fly and jump. It's my freedom, my joy."

"Who said you had to give it up to make a commitment? And who asked you to make any commitment?"

"Connie, you can tell how things are going. I. . .can't help myself when I'm around you. And the last thing in the world I want to do is hurt you."

"I see. Well, just walk on off then, Maury Donovan. Now. I don't understand why we're having this conversation. In case you think for some bizarre reason that I have some sort of feeling for you and you were about to hurt me, you can think again. I can take care of myself. And if you don't mind, *sir*, I'd like to finish this walk by myself. . . ."

"Connie!" He grabbed her arm, she jerked it away. "Connie, I'm sorry if I said that all wrong. Look, I'm a big dunce."

"Yes, you are! For once you're absolutely right. You're a dunce because you think you can get away from commitments by hanging between earth and sky. Well, you can't!"

BRENDA KNIGHT GRAHAM, a Georgia native, is an active volunteer in her church and community. She has written several books for both adults and children, but this is her first novel for **Heartsong Presents**.

On Wings of Song

Brenda Knight Graham

To Aunt Emma
Thanks for being the
wonderful person
you are!
Love,
Brenda

Heartsong Presents

A note from the Author:

Dedicated to Charles—
"More today than yesterday,
less today than tomorrow."

I would like to thank the following who were so helpful
when I was writing this book: Virginia Bonnette,
Suzanne, Fairlight, and Rebecca Dover, John Knight,
and Eric Peck. Thanks, Charles, for that hike into
Tallulah Gorge!

I love to hear from my readers! You may write to me at
the following address: **Brenda Knight Graham**
Author Relations
P.O. Box 719
Uhrichsville, OH 44683

ISBN 1-55748-860-6

ON WINGS OF SONG

Cover illustration by Kay Salem.

PRINTED IN THE U.S.A.

one

Connie Jensen looked up from writing in her bright new record book to scan the little faces of her eighteen students and try to connect names with them. She had given them each an art assignment. Some weren't paying it much attention while others puzzled over blank sheets and a few plied crayons or pencils with feverish zeal, shoulders hunched over their desks.

There was Marie, such a pretty little girl, but with straggly, dirty hair; Sammy Craven, clean and shining with a mother's obvious care; Richard with his tongue at the side of his mouth as he toiled with his pencil. Connie had so looked forward to this very day, finally having her own class of children, though she hadn't really planned on first graders. She simply wouldn't let anything put a stopper on her joy, not Mr. Donovan with his strict ultimatums nor Zena Furr, fellow teacher, with her negative predictions.

She would teach these children to read! In a glow of romanticism she pictured herself surrounded by bright-eyed children, maybe sitting on a big rug with them all looking up to her, all excited as it came their turn to read from crisp new books.

It might be hard for a few weeks to prove to Mr. Maury Donovan, Pine Ridge Elementary's principal, that she could teach retained first graders and slow second graders as well or better than anybody. But he would see very soon that just because it was her first year teaching did not mean she was incompetent.

She couldn't help it that Mr. Donovan was out of his office the day she was hired, nor could she help it that the school board chose to hire her for this Georgia mountain school without his consultation. And she certainly couldn't help it that he seemed to resent her—as an impostor maybe? Her home in Augusta was only three hours away. He'd asked her why she hadn't stayed nearer home her first year teaching—as if she needed to hold her mother's hand or something.

But she wasn't going to hold her mother's hand and she didn't intend to hold anyone's hand. Right now she didn't even want her fiancé, Henry Segars, suggesting all the time what she should do. Which was the whole reason for her being here, she supposed, to get away from Henry. She felt smothered by him somehow, and she had to get some perspective on things before they married. She had to know she really loved him.

A cracking snap interrupted the room's studious hum as a boy near the door broke his pencil. It wasn't just the lead that broke, but the whole pencil popped right in the middle. She wouldn't have believed it on little Marie's word alone, but she turned her head in time to see the boy laying the pieces down side by side with a look of near pride in his otherwise blank face. The kid certainly had strength in his hands. She ran her finger down her class roll. That was Rob Fenton, a retained first grader. Zena, teacher of the other first grade class, had already warned her he would never learn to read or write.

Before she could go see about Rob, two little girls stood at her desk, puzzled looks on their faces.

"Miss Jensen, what d'ya mean draw somethin' we like to do? I can't draw nothin'."

"Me neither," said the other.

"I just mean make a picture. Don't you like to make pictures?"

"No, ma'am. Don't know how. You gone show us?"

"Well. All right. Suppose I really, really like flying kites. Well, actually I do like flying kites so it's not just supposing. I'll draw a girl out in a big, big wide pasture. Let's give her some long hair blowing in the wind. Like this. Now. She's holding a string and at the end of that string a diamond-shaped kite's flying way up in the sky. You see? Now that wasn't hard. What do *you* like to do?"

"Mostly watch TV."

"And maybe have hamburgers," said the second little brown-eyed girl.

Groaning within, Connie flipped her long silky black hair out of her face, smiled at the little girls, and said, "There, you see? Make a picture of what you just told me. Watching TV and eating hamburgers. You can do that. And don't forget the ketchup."

Mr. Donovan had made it very clear he wanted a minimum of art and music presented to the first three grades at Pine Ridge Elementary School. That meant leaving art and music to the special teachers who came to Pine Ridge twice a week for forty minutes with each class. He didn't approve of classroom teachers using what he called frivolous activities to teach mathematical facts and reading skills. He said the activities themselves would get all the children's attention. She hoped he'd soon realize that children absorb through all senses, the more the better.

She knew literacy was still a major problem in affluent America, even after computers and all kinds of modern methods had been tried. Now there was a big drive to go "back to the basics." But that didn't mean forget all that had been learned about child psychology, did it? Connie wondered just how much Mr. Donovan really knew about how to motivate children. As young as he was, he couldn't have been out of school more than ten years.

Yet there seemed a wider gap for some reason. Instead of his seeming too young to be a principal—which his looks would imply—he almost seemed too old! A principal was supposed to be a leader of teachers, wasn't he? Hadn't Mother always bragged about how her principal gave teachers a chance to suggest and object? Mr. Donovan was more of a narrow-minded squelcher!

"Our main aim is to teach these children how to read," Mr. Donovan had said at a teachers' meeting, pounding his fist for emphasis.

Even now Connie felt the sting of disapproval in his blue stare when she'd raised her hand and objected to his minimizing the use of music and art. He didn't stare long. He barked back at her that these children *were* going to learn to read, as if she'd intended anything different, and that leaving off extraneous subjects was the way he would make sure of it. She glanced at the other teachers. Could they really be as placid and agreeable as they all looked?

Mr. Donovan was a large man with a deep voice and his eyes. . . . Well, if he weren't so horrible, she'd have thought they were beautiful, such a deep blue in his tanned face. No one could deny he was a striking man as handsome went. But already he'd lived up to Mrs. Haburn's warnings to Connie. Connie's landlady had said for Connie to wear her armor at all times because Mr. Donovan, a former air force pilot, was apt to run his school like a military camp.

Connie wondered if it wasn't a case of "bark worse than bite" and planned to go right ahead *using* music and art to teach reading. It would be fun and exciting for the children, and they would learn fast. She wasn't planning to make teachers such as Zena feel bad about having failed these same children last year. She only planned to motivate the boys and girls to the point that, by Christmas, everyone, especially the children themselves, would wonder if it could be the same class.

All her life Connie had known she would be a teacher. Even at the age of eight she and some cousins had played school under her grandparents' house in Aiken, S.C. Remembering, she could smell the mossy dankness, feel the smart when she whacked her head against a floor sill, and the humiliation when Grandmother shooed them out for pestering her favorite laying hen. Connie, always taller by inches than her peers, was given much credit for being "responsible," which was often a burden since hers was the name shouted in exasperation when they got into mischief. But she, nearly always the teacher, did enjoy quizzing her cousins in spelling and sums.

Now she knew there was so much more to teaching

than quizzing. Like getting to know how her students thought—her motive behind this present assignment. Connie fluffed wrinkles out of her cotton skirt as she went around her desk and proceeded to peer over her students' shoulders, viewing their pictures. All in all, what she saw was amazing, though perhaps not helpful in character analysis—hamburgers, televisions, stick trees, and people with oversized feet and ears. But Marie had drawn herself swinging. Connie smiled at the great amount of hair the little girl had put on herself. She looked up at Connie and whispered, "I made my hair like yours." Connie promised herself as she moved on that soon she would wash Marie's hair.

Sammy Craven was only doodling on his paper and put his hands over it quickly as she approached. But Richard. . .why, Richard's picture had a house, a dog, a truck with a child riding in the back. Really good images.

"You like to ride in your father's truck?" she asked and was rewarded only with a shy, lopsided grin that didn't say anything.

Connie checked her roll one more time before writing down her attendance count. One boy, Billy Ray Spence was missing. Somebody at preplanning had said something about the Spences. Oh, yes, it was Mrs. Gurdy, the wide teacher who wore hats to school. She'd said watch out for the Spences.

There were several Spence families represented at Pine Ridge and the children were absent a lot, but when they were there they were troublemakers. If one were picked on by another student and his brother, sister, or cousin found out about it there usually were consequences. Nothing really terrible had happened, but several children had been bruised up by fighting Spences.

Connie stole a look at Richard, still bent over his picture. He was a Spence, too, but she couldn't imagine him in a fight.

"No, Rob!" she said, suddenly hurrying from behind her desk, but not in time to stop that child from deliberately breaking a little girl's pencil. She took him gently to a corner and explained timeout to him.

Rob followed her back to her desk. While she was in the midst of explaining to him again why he should stand in the corner, the door flew open and in walked Mr. Donovan, towering over a squirming boy he held by his collar, a scowling boy with his hair sticking out over the tops of his ears. Though blood was trickling down over the boy's lips, his expression defied any sympathy.

"Miss Jensen, this is Billy Ray Spence. He had a fight on the bus this morning and now, as you see, has a substantial nosebleed. Do you think you can handle this?"

She wasn't sure whether he was challenging her, almost with glee, or anxious that all go well. Either way she bristled at the implication she might *not* be able to handle it, even if her stomach were churning at the smell of sweat and blood. "Of course! Go to your desk, Billy Ray, and put your head back. I'll bring cool paper towels. Thank you, Mr. Donovan. I'll take it from here."

"Are you sure?"

"Yes, I'm sure."

She showed Billy Ray how to hold a wet paper towel with a firm pressure against his upper lip and went about

trying to get Rob to stay in one place. It was apparent
that a timeout corner wasn't going to mean anything to
him, but she had to find some way of keeping him occupied. How could she teach anyone in the room with Rob
wandering all about pulling hair and breaking pencils?
A whimper of, "Teacher, teacher" followed him around
the room.

She finally gave him a lump of modeling clay and told
him he had to stay at his desk to play with it. Praying he
would, she hurried back to Billy Ray. The bleeding was
stopped. He'd wadded the bloody towels up and thrown
them toward the trash, missing it by a mile. She looked
at him, then the wadded towels, and decided not to discuss trash right now.

"Billy Ray, I've asked everyone to make a picture to
start with this morning, a picture of something you like
to do. I want you to draw it on this paper with your pencil. I'll give you a little more time while the rest of us get
started on a reading lesson."

He tore the paper in two pieces, wadded each of them,
and threw them toward the trash. "I don't make pictures,"
he said. "My cousin, Richard, makes pictures. I make
bloody noses."

She wanted to laugh, but managed not to. "Billy Ray!"
she said in the most authoritative voice she could mus-
ter. "I do not allow behavior like that in my room."

"Good," said the boy, both fists balled tightly where
they lay on his desk. "Then tell them 'at makes me come
to leave me alone. I'll stay to home."

"I'll do no such thing, and you'll straighten that back
of yours like a brave boy and show me you know how to

learn. Now here's another paper. Please get started."

Her knees were quivering as she went back to her desk and began talking to the class about the letter "A." But she thought she'd have no more trouble with Billy Ray. She was wrong. When she went to pick up his picture, she was horrified. No wonder he'd had to sharpen his pencil several times. He'd covered the whole sheet with a black screen punctuated by stabbed holes. "That's what I like to do," he said, shoving the paper at her. "I like to make things go black."

❧

Connie's head ached dully as she left the building that afternoon and crawled into her car. As she tooled around curves going north to Mrs. Haburn's, she began to feel a little better. The mountains were still there in spite of her hectic day, the blue mountains with autumn reds beginning to stain saddlebacks and ridges. From one high curve she looked down on a little valley populated with a white house, a big brown barn, rows of apple trees, and a bright green pasture where black cows grazed, confined within a white-posted fence. But even better than those storybook scenes were the wild ones like the old rusty gate twined by a brilliant red vine, or the small waterfall rushing from dark woods to catapult down a black rock face, roaring like a baby lion.

She felt much better by the time she turned off the Clayton Highway into Mrs. Haburn's driveway, which plunged steeply down to the pond, ran along beside it a moment, then rushed upward again to stop by her screened-in porch where an orange and white cat was giving himself a leisurely bath. As Connie tugged her books and supplies out of the seat, the screen door slammed and Mrs. Haburn herself, walking with her usual decided limp, bumped down the steps, lugging an armload of odd items.

"Go put your things up and get changed," she ordered with a smile almost as wide as her hat. "We're goin' fishin', an' I don't want no argument. I've even got us a snack here 'mongst all this stuff. Hurry and change. You look plumb tuckered out. Oh, and those telephone messages can wait. Henry said you could call him tonight, and Mr. Donovan can sure wait a little while."

"Mr. Donovan called?"

"Yeah, but don't you worry. You go put on them jeans an' come on down. I'm gonna teach you how to catch a fish."

Connie looked past Mrs. Haburn's squat waddling figure to the rippling pond that reflected clumps of bulrushes, a little rugged dock, and a cloud-flecked blue sky. Beyond the pond, blueberry bushes ambled in crooked rows, their zillions of tiny leaves a rich wine red. The hill that banked behind them was in shadow now, but dogwoods and maples flamed red amongst the pines.

Yes, she'd go fishing.

First, she tried to call Mr. Donovan, but his line was busy and she dashed on out. The afternoon was too gorgeous to waste. As she ran down toward the pond with wind whipping hair away from her face, she tried to forget Mr. Donovan's stern look of disapproval and doubt when he brought Billy Ray to her classroom.

two

Connie munched happily on a sweet little Yate apple while Mrs. Haburn baited and rebaited her hook, splashing more and more fish into her bucket. As long as she kept eating, Connie reasoned, Mrs. Haburn wouldn't bug her to try a hand at fishing. Connie looked down between her dangling feet to her reflection in the murky pond. A cloud of dark hair around a blob of white face was about all she could see.

"What were you telling me about this apple, Mrs. Haburn? You caught a fish about that time and forgot to finish your story."

"Oh. I'm bad about that. Not finishin' things I start. I was just sayin' my papa owned a great orchard an' he prided himself on growin' old-fashioned apples. Taste of a good tart or sweet apple brings back the good ole days like nothin' else. I like Jonathans and Yates the best. When the farm sold after he died, I dug up a few of his knee-high trees so's I could grow my own little orchard. Over yonder, back of the blueberries.

"The trees are good bearers. An' real popular. All I have to do is set up a table with small baskets of apples by the road and afore noon I'll have sold 'em, every one. That's a busy road there. My blueberry sign does the trick for me in July, too. Everybody around loves my blueberries. They're sweeter'n most, freeze good, too. 'Course in fall o' year, when color's at its peak, it's hard to get onto this road and that's pretty aggravatin', you know.

"I don't worry too much, since I don't drive anyway and don't have a car. But I have to worry for my drivers. The Lord sure were good to send you, Connie Jensen. When you said you'd pay part of your rent by runnin' me for groceries, to the doctor, and 'specially to church every Sunday, I could have stood on my head. There now, that's the kind of fish I were alookin' fer."

Mrs. Haburn flopped an eight-inch catfish within a foot of Connie. While Connie scrambled up, the older woman chuckled low in her throat. "You can throw that core you've done wore out into the water, hon. The fish'll eat it right up. Then you'll have a hand to get that fish off the hook for me."

There was a pause. Mrs. Haburn peered around at Connie's face and promptly began pulling the fish toward herself. "Or, then again, maybe I'll do it myself. Here, just let me get that other pole goin' fer you now. It's time you drowned a few worms. You gotta have somethin' pleasant to tell your Henry tonight, ain't ye?"

Connie giggled softly, knowing full well Mrs. Haburn was trying to get her to start talking about Henry. What *would* she tell Henry tonight? She could tell him about Richard's nice picture, about Marie's sweet nature, about Zena, her new teacher friend, and about that adorable, neat little girl named Joyce who wanted to mother everyone, even Billy Ray. Except she didn't want to talk to Henry about Billy Ray.

It was funny that she never wanted to talk to Henry about problems. She didn't know why. He wasn't an unkind person, certainly. He just never seemed quite able to understand. Probably because he didn't have problems himself.

"I were afraid you mightn't be a very good fisherman, being from the city," Mrs. Haburn commented as she threaded a worm onto a hook. She showed Connie how to toss it in and watch the cork set itself upright in the middle of multiplying ripple rings.

Connie jerked herself out of a daze just in time to clutch the pole as the cork began to swirl and dive. She wanted to dislodge Mrs. Haburn's preconceived ideas about her. But after losing her bait several times and, worse, catching a pearl gray fish and being totally unable to touch it, Connie was convinced Mrs. Haburn was right about her. She laid down her pole and watched her landlady, who sat flat on the dock with big boots stuck out before her, pulling in a hefty mess.

"Mrs. Haburn, what will you do with all these fish?"

"Oh, maybe have my whole church to supper one night. That Henry of yours might even be there. And you needn't be so shy. I do have eyes, you know, an' I've been watchin' that fine ring of yours turn sun rays into rainbows."

Connie's frown turned to laughter. "Mrs. Haburn, you should have had a dozen children for all your energy and mothering instinct."

"I'd a'sure taken a dozen if they'd a'come. But me an' my ole man only got two. I guess that's just all the Lord trusted us with."

"You really set a lot of store on what the Lord thinks about everything, don't you, Mrs. Haburn."

"Of course. Don't you?"

"Well, not as much as you, I guess." Connie placed

her hands, palms down, behind her and leaned back to look up at the sky fringed by hills on either side. Far overhead a tiny jet raced ahead of its stream of vapor, and a minute later its own sound droned along, trying to catch up.

"Sometimes I wish I were more dedicated," she continued. "More. . .more sure of what God's like and everything. I mean, I'm going to heaven. I know that. But people like you who are so happy right now make me wonder if I'm missing something."

Mrs. Haburn began winding in the fishing lines. "If you are missin' somethin'," she said, "you'll find it. If you search for it with all your heart, Lord always meets you halfway. Are you gonna come with me to church on Sundays?"

"I. . .sometimes maybe. But. . ." Connie didn't know exactly how to tell Mrs. Haburn she wanted to be left alone. She didn't mind taking her places. That was their deal. But she didn't intend to be involved in everything Mrs. Haburn did. She was only her chauffeur. Mrs. Haburn must have read her mind. The woman was uncanny!

"You have many other things to do, I know. I know, hon. But it would please me very much. My own children are both way up there in Maine, you know. Why they both had to go so far is beyond me, but they're happy where they are. Anyway, give me a hand here. My, my, there's a chill in that air, don't you think? Let's get these things put up and set out some supper. I put a pot roast on an' it should be just about gettin' tender."

Later, Connie showered, wrapped her head in a towel, and, tucked warmly into a soft terry robe, stood as near her room door as the hallway phone would reach as she returned her calls. She hoped Mrs. Haburn would be so busy at her crocheting that she wouldn't listen to her.

First, Mr. Maury Donovan. Might as well get it over with. She tensed as she heard the ring at the other end of the line, relaxed as it rang over and over with no answer, and finally laughed softly to herself with relief. But of course, this was the school number and Mr. Donovan would have gone home long since. And he wouldn't have intended her to call him at home. Probably was nothing that couldn't wait till morning anyway.

She dialed Henry's number and instantly could see his dear solid self, dressed in a suit and tie and smelling of cologne. Well, no, he'd have changed by now into tee shirt and shorts. She glanced at her watch. Good. It was 7:30. His favorite newscast was over.

She tried to sound eager as she answered his questions about her first day at school. But the eagerness in her voice had only to do with her children, not with Henry. She stared down at her ring, beautiful even in this dark corner, as she listened to his soft voice begging her to break her contract and come on home. She was touched. It wasn't like Henry, who was always so organized and together, to be begging.

But she couldn't relent. She would not give up this chance to be herself. And so, again and again, she heard herself saying, "Henry, no. I can't, Henry. It's only for a year, you know. You're so busy with your job at the bank anyway, you'll hardly miss me once you get used to it. Just wait and see."

"Persistent, ain't he?" spoke Mrs. Haburn from her comfortable chair in the den, when she heard the phone click into place.

"Mrs. Haburn! Please! Don't eavesdrop!" Connie tried to hold back some of her irritation, but it wasn't easy.

"Why, my dear, what can you expect with both of us livin' in this snug little house? You don't expect me not to care what happens to you, do you?"

"Care, yes. But meddle, no! I came here—"

"To get away from meddlin'? Well, I'll try to be good. But. . ." She adjusted the folds of the afghan she was creating and smiled up at Connie, who'd come to stand over her, hands on hips. "I'll try to be good," she finished lamely, seeing Connie was really not being funny at all.

❧

There was a peremptory note on Connie's door when she got to school the next morning. Mr. Maury Donovan wanted to see her in his office. Well, she wanted to see him, too. She wanted to talk to him about Rob Fenton. Surely she hadn't been hired to be a baby sitter!

Thinking of this helped her square her shoulders as she spoke to his secretary and entered the principal's office, only to find Mr. Donovan busy on the phone. He barely acknowledged her with an uplifted finger. She paced, irritated at having to wait when there was so much for her to do. There were those reading activity sheets to copy before school, and she wanted to rearrange the desks into a big circle instead of rows, and wet a big sponge for children to "plant" rye seeds on. She itched to get started!

Finally she sat down on a leather chair and took a minute to look at Mr. Donovan's diplomas and military awards. Somehow she was surprised to also see beautiful sky pictures—sunsets, a full moon with a pine bough brushing it, and one bright photo of sky divers coming down in formation. Maybe she'd misjudged the man. He couldn't be hardhearted and like such beauty, could he? Then she noticed a small photo, a close-up of. . .could that be Mr. Donovan? She stood to inspect it more closely. It *was* Mr. Donovan! He was dressed in sky diving clothes, wearing the most radiant smile. Connie looked at it and then at the man now scowling into the telephone. They couldn't be the same person. But they were. She started visibly as his voice raked across her shoulder.

"Miss Jensen, I called you in because I felt we had a few points that might need clearing up. Sorry to keep you waiting. This won't take long."

She faced him, telling herself, *Stand straight now for the firing squad.*

Mr. Donovan looked at her hard, then shook his head as if to rid himself of a fly.

"For one thing," he continued, "the next time I leave word for you to call I would appreciate your responding promptly."

"Yes, sir." She spoke automatically and then flushed in fury at being humiliated. This was to be nothing but an old-fashioned lecture.

"As to what I was calling about. . . ." He had come around his desk to stand before her and she had to will herself not to move back a step. She wouldn't let him know he intimidated her that way, that his very large-ness fairly took her breath away. "I perceive you don't agree with my methods, Miss Jensen. In fact, I feel you were defying me by starting out your class with artwork, however simple, after I specifically demanded you leave art and music to the time slots allotted to them. I know you disagree and you have a right to your own opinions. But only your opinions. I'm principal here. And I will not tolerate having my rules blatantly ignored. Life will be much more pleasant for both of us if you recognize that and simply follow my instructions."

She had tried to keep eye contact. She felt that was very important in being respectful to him as well as to herself. But somewhere along the way she began seeing his face as it was in that little picture and something about the contrast was so comical it was all she could do to keep from laughing. She had to drop her eyes, and when she did she saw his beat-up tennis shoes, wet with dew. The man was wearing nice slacks and a sport coat, but those shoes. . . . She couldn't resist smiling.

"Miss Jensen, why do I get the feeling you're not listening to me?"

His eyes were stern and hard when she looked up. She flashed him a brilliant smile.

"Mr. Donovan, I've heard every word. I'll try my best to abide by. . .your rules. But I wish you'd reconsider. The children so need—"

He was opening the door. He was showing her out! Her cheeks stung with angry warmth as she struggled to be polite, wishing him a good day. Suddenly she remembered her own request and spun back around.

"What about Rob Fenton, Mr. Donovan? He's obviously mentally challenged and needs to be in a special class. Surely he's not going to be in my room all year!" Now that's not the way she'd meant to say it. But it was out now.

"No, Miss Jensen, he is not. Only for half of each day.

He will be bused to another school where his special education teacher has a room. But the board hired her late, and we've been asked to give her a week's preparation time. Don't tell me one day has done you in, Miss Jensen?"

She caught her bottom lip between her teeth for a second. So, she really did have a lot to learn and he knew it.

"I. . .I'm sorry. Of course it's no problem. I was only concerned about the child. Mr. Donovan, if I could just use some art with Rob. . .and Billy Ray."

Mr. Donovan's jaw tensed. "No art, Miss Jensen. I don't expect a miracle with Rob Fenton. But I do expect the rest of your children to be reading by the first of the year." He was all but shaking a big finger in her face!

She willed her voice to stay steady, though her eyes glinted with dangerous lightning. "You mean you've given up on Rob Fenton? I think I could teach him some skills if I were allowed to use—"

"I don't give up on anyone!" he shouted, then turned and raked a hand through his hair as if he were remembering something. Heading for his desk, he said over his shoulder, "Miss Jensen, please let me know if there's anything within the parameters I've laid out that my office can do to help you. Now, if you will excuse me, my phone is ringing."

When the door closed on her, Connie wanted to beat on it, but instead she turned down the hallway toward her room, mimicking him as she mumbled, "The parameters I've laid out."

Zena appeared beside her, falling in with her fast stride. "Boss got to you this morning, huh?"

"He sure did."

"Well, don't let it eat on you. He's that way. Some days are worse than others. You'll learn how to get along without crossing him."

"I'm not sure I want to. He needs to be crossed. He's all wrong. Children need to *like* learning, Zena."

"Oh, Connie, that's just stuff they teach you in those education classes. It doesn't work in the real world. You have to do what the principal says, or after a year of misery, you'll be out!" Zena made a slash across her own throat with one finger to illustrate her point.

"And let me give you another bit of advice. Not that you look very interested right now. And I know you're wearing an engagement ring, too. But just in case, don't get any romantic ideas about Mr. Donovan because he's only interested in light relationships. I should know."

In total surprise, Connie turned toward the wispy little blond. "You?"

"Yes, I went out with him a few times last year. And he was a perfect gentleman. But, believe me, he doesn't intend for anyone to get near that heart of his. So save yourself some pain, okay?"

Connie unlocked her classroom door, shaking her head. So strange. She'd never dreamed of having any romantic ideas about that man. Heaven forbid! Right now she heartily wished she'd stayed in Augusta, Georgia.

three

From her bed, Connie watched the very early Sunday morning light reveal the character of her corner room. She could hardly believe how right she felt about this room in only a few weeks. . .its scents, textures, bright pillows in a chair by the window, everything.

There was an abundance of space for books, even in her bedstead. The bed had belonged to one of Mrs. Haburn's children and the headboard doubled as a bookcase. A desk of some dark wood topped with shelves nearly as high as the ceiling occupied one wall, while near the door a corner cabinet cozied into a space it didn't exactly fit. She eyed the cabinet and the corner and decided one of them at least was a bit crooked.

The room lightened some more, and Connie could study the new wallpaper job, which left a lot to be desired in the way of perfection since, as Mrs. Haburn had put it, her young friends from church had "thrown it up for me one weekend." Connie smiled at the video that played through her brain of many hands at work that had never before attempted the skill of papering around windows and light sockets.

Her attention turned to a favorite focus in the room, a picture of a couple, praying in a field, a pitchfork stuck in the ground by the man who held his hat reverently in front of him. Behind the woman, who wore a long dress and apron, was a wooden wheelbarrow piled high with hay. She also was bowed in prayer. It was a familiar piece of art, but Connie couldn't remember the name of it. "Evening Prayers?" She'd have to ask Mrs. Haburn. That lady had offered to take it down so Connie could have the space for hanging her own choice of picture, but so far she hadn't wanted to replace it.

The picture was so peaceful, so inspiring, so like what Mrs. Haburn would choose to hang. Already she'd invited Connie to pray with her each morning "to get her day off to a good start." At first Connie was hesitant, not wanting to be held to such a rigorous morning schedule. But Mrs. Haburn was so sweet and persuasive, she decided she could at least do it for a while. The little woman was so energetic she put Connie to shame. She was up cooking breakfast no matter how early Connie got up, was constantly making applesauce and canning it or trundling a wheelbarrow of leaves to a mulch pile. And when Connie got home from school, often Mrs. Haburn was up by the road, vigorously selling apples, extolling their goodness as if they were made of pure gold.

Sunlight patterned leaf shapes against Connie's curtains, maple leaves that she knew were turning red, but seen through the curtains were only shifting shadows on blue cotton. Suddenly she sat upright, then ran to her front window to pull back the curtain and peer through the maple tree to the steep hillside rising from the other side of the road. Gauzy vapor clung in low spots between house and road and Connie caught her breath as she spied a rabbit sitting not twenty feet from her window, nibbling on some grass.

"I've got to get out of here and see everything," she breathed to herself. "I bet the pond is gorgeous about now."

As she slid into jeans and tee shirt, she could hear Mrs. Haburn talking. *Must be on the phone,* she thought. Maybe she could slip past her unnoticed.

But Mrs. Haburn wasn't on the phone. She was talking to a smoky little fire she'd started in her kitchen heater. Though she was bent over, prodding a weak flame as Connie crept by, she called out cheerily, "Have you some breakfast in no time, dearie. This fire's for comfort, you know, not cookin'. You go on and have yourself a little walk an' when you get back I'll have you some pancakes an' coffee. You like sorghum? Don't know? Well, you'll be for findin' out soon. Have a nice walk now, you hear?"

Connie made a wry face as she left the house, the cat trailing along behind her. Couldn't she move around here without being noticed? But Mrs. Haburn was so kind, too.

Shaking her head as if to clear her mind of such thoughts, Connie explored the hillside beyond the pond. She sat down on an old log, while the cat stalked little creatures and played in the noisy leaves.

She knew she'd done the right thing coming to this community, choosing this "jumping off place," as Daddy called it, for a home. Yes, even taking the job at Pine Ridge seemed a good idea right now, in spite of Mr. Maury Donovan. But still she had such an unsettled feeling. If Henry wasn't the one for her, then who was? And, after all, *could* she be a good teacher?

As she idly pulled bits of bark off her sitting log and tossed them teasingly at the cat, she wondered what it would be like to be really at peace with your world like the couple in Mrs. Haburn's picture or like Mrs. Haburn herself.

Lord, I really want to be the person You planned me to be. I really do. Connie rubbed goose bumps on her arms and started back down to the pond.

Vapor hovered close over the water with a silvery, eerie appearance. Connie ambled along, enjoying the smells of bulrushes, dewy grass, and some unnameable spicy scent that seemed to come with autumn. The cat pounced on something that turned out to be a little frog. Connie knelt to inspect the victim. Pitying him, she threw him back into the pond, hoping he'd survive, though part of one leg was gone. Watching the perfectly symmetrical circles twinkle outward from where he'd splashed in, she suddenly wondered if he'd been a toad instead of a frog. *I may be more dangerous as an ecological sympathizer than to ignore it all and let it fix itself!*

When she got back, pancakes and coffee were ready. They had never tasted so good. Maybe it was the sorghum.

Mrs. Haburn rubbed her hands together in childish excitement and exclaimed, "I just know this is the day you're going to church with me. I just know it!"

"Well, actually. . ." Connie hadn't planned to go. She really wanted time alone. But her going seemed to mean so much to Mrs. Haburn. This little woman was so bright-eyed and so wistful and had already asked several times. The least she could do was go to church with her. And it couldn't help but be good for her. "Yes, I'll go with you this time," she answered cautiously.

Mrs. Haburn ignored the caution and began vigorously to clear the table. "I can't wait for you to hear Reverend Stone. I know you're gonna like him a lot. He an' Mrs. Stone aren't that much older than you, an' they're simply the dearest people. Don't know how to discipline their own children, but other than that they're really fine.

"Reverend Stone wants us all to call him Phil, but you know, I just can't do that. He's the age of my own boy, or younger, but I can't feel right calling my preacher Phil. That just ain't right. But all the young folks do, you know. Next thing, the way everyone's demanding this right an' that an' changin' old traditions, school teachers won't even be called Miss or Mrs. anymore."

Connie had to laugh at Mrs. Haburn's wonderful grumbling good cheer. "Oh, that'll be the day, Mrs. Haburn. With concerned citizens like you still around, I doubt that'll happen."

&

The church was charming, a white frame building with a steeple pointing to a sky which, that day, was bluer than any Connie thought she'd ever seen. It was only about three miles on toward Clayton from Mrs. Haburn's house and was atop a small hill, like a beacon for all to see.

"I raised my children in this little church," rattled Mrs. Haburn gathering her Bible and Sunday school book and hunting for the door handle as Connie turned off the ignition. "We got married here and here's where my husband's buried. It's a pretty important place in our lives. Well, I know the building itself ain't the church, but it is pretty special, you know. Well, anyways, here we are."

Connie persuaded Mrs. Haburn to let her sit in on her own Bible study class that first time. "I don't know a soul here but you, and I came to church to be with you," she insisted.

"You need to make acquaintance with other young folks," said Mrs. Haburn over and over, but finally she agreed.

Connie was almost overwhelmed with questions by Mrs. Haburn's friends. It wasn't just her life history they wanted, she grinned to herself when finally she and Mrs. Haburn were seated in church. They'd have wanted her great-grandfather's history if she'd known it. Mrs. Haburn was mild beside some of them.

She peered sideways at her landlady just in time to catch Mrs. Haburn winking, then flashing a beaming smile toward the pulpit. Expecting to see Mrs. Haburn's beloved Reverend Stone, Connie looked up, too just in time to lock eyes with the distinctly startled, deep blue eyes of Maury Donovan, the minister of music, as he announced an opening hymn.

She looked swiftly at Mrs. Haburn, but she was innocently searching for the hymn number in her book, the little devious woman. She knew if she'd told Connie who was directing music she'd have never come!

Connie tried not to look at him. But how could she sing joyfully without looking up at the leader? Every time she did, there was Maury Donovan, an astonishing Maury Donovan. She could not believe what was happening. This Mr. Donovan was nothing like the man she met every morning at school, scowling his way along the corridors, shaking his big finger, and passing down rule after rule.

This Mr. Donovan was glowing, yes, positively glowing with happy energy as they sang "He Keeps Me Singing." He really and truly looked as if he believed totally what he was singing. But how could he possibly believe that "Jesus swept across the broken strings, Stirred the slumb'ring chords again" when he went about making everyone miserable all week?

She was relieved when the singing was over and the big disturbing figure of Maury Donovan, resplendent in suit and tie, settled himself on the front pew with a row of wiggling little boys. Now she could listen to the little preacher Mrs. Haburn had talked about so much.

Or could she? She had to keep pulling herself back from thinking about the strange double life of Maury Donovan as she tried to hear Reverend Stone's sermon, his first in a series on the Beatitudes. She could see how Mrs. Haburn liked the man. He was so warm, eloquent, and down-to-earth, so humble, and yet so confident.

She wished she were a better listener. And she would have been, she knew full well, if it hadn't been for that looming set of shoulders in a dark gray suit on the front row, the dark head often bent to whisper to a little boy beside him. It wasn't fair that he was in this part of her world, too.

But she didn't have to come to church with Mrs. Haburn. She'd just go elsewhere. But why should she? Why should it matter one way or the other? She looked down at her ring, twisted it to make rainbows gleam in a ray of sunshine coming through one of the many tall windows. Why wasn't she sitting securely in church with Henry right this minute?

Oh, Lord, please help me concentrate on worshiping You. And don't let me get addled over that aggravating man!

"So good to have you with us today, Connie," said Reverend Stone as Mrs. Haburn introduced them after the service. "Mrs. Haburn's like a mom to a bunch of us, and her friends are our friends. Sure hope you like us. Say, we're like a big family around here and some of us nearly always go out to eat after church. How about you and Mrs. Haburn joining us, hmmm? We're going toward Toccoa today to a friendly barbecue place. We'd like it if you'd come."

"Well, really, that's very kind of you, but I thought—"

"You know, Connie, that's not a bad idea," piped up Mrs. Haburn at her elbow, "seein' as how I never got any dinner cooked before we left. We'd only have a sandwich if we went on home. That'd be too bad now, wouldn't it?"

The woman was insufferable! Connie's mouth dropped open and Mrs. Haburn nodded with Reverend Stone as if that was a sure assent. So before Connie knew what was happening, she and Mrs. Haburn were being ushered to the church van where, of all the downright impossible situations, Connie had no choice but to sit beside Maury Donovan. Since there were too many passengers in the van, the seating was very tight, and Connie squirmed against the unforgiving window, wondering why she'd allowed herself to be persuaded like soft butter, led away like a starving stray or some such awful figure of speech. She vowed she'd never again let Mrs. Haburn talk her into anything.

Mr. Donovan put his arm loosely around her as he talked to a young woman on his other side. He was totally unconscious of her, yet she was so uncomfortable that her palms were sweating and she decided she'd concentrate on Mrs. Haburn. She could see Mrs. Haburn's peppery hair bobbing just in front of her as she talked loudly with Reverend Stone. The preacher was driving and one of his sons was talking to him at the same time, but he never missed a bit of what Mrs. Haburn was telling him about one time when she had chickens and a fox got in her henhouse and couldn't get back out before the chickens pecked his eyes out.

"Some kind of justice there," laughed Phil Stone to his wife, Margie. There was a general babble as the van traveled to the other side of what Phil Stone said was Mile Long Hill, a long steep stretch down into a V and back up as high again. Ed's Barbecue was set among some pines, a simple structure with no great view or claim of atmosphere. "Just plain good food," said Dave Olds, a young man who gallantly offered to help Mrs. Haburn out of the van.

If Mr. Donovan had even looked at her the whole trip, Connie wasn't aware of it. But now, as they both waited to climb out of the van, he turned to her, his eyes demanding her full attention. Was there a hint of amusement twinkling in their blue depths and tickling at the corners of that wide mouth? She smiled uncertainly. For one moment she actually had the feeling she was going to reach up and brush strands of hair back from his forehead, but thankfully her arm was pinned so tightly she couldn't impulsively commit such an awful goof.

"Sorry about the tight quarters here, Miss uhm, Miss Jensen, I believe it is? Good thing it's no farther or you might have disappeared into that crack. Mrs. Haburn, what are you feeding your boarder, ghost rations?"

Was he patronizing her or trying to be funny? Either way he'd failed. She couldn't think of anything to reply and was saved the trouble by the young Stones, demanding that Mr. Donovan please, please sit with them in the restaurant. There they appeared to have one hilarious time telling jokes and corny riddles.

From the table where Connie sat near a large buck stove, it seemed Maury Donovan was having the most fun of anyone. His spontaneous laughter escaped in sudden roars and drew everyone else to it as cats are attracted to heat. He couldn't help laughing, and no one else could resist laughing with him. Except Connie, who resisted pretty well. If there was anything she hated worse than a cranky person, it was a hypocrite in any form, and that's evidently what this Maury Donovan was. If he had such a sanguine personality, why did he keep it hidden under a cloak of pessimism at Pine Ridge Elementary?

Phil Stone got up and walked among the tables, talking not only to members of their party but to other diners as well. Was there anyone the man didn't know? One might have mistaken him for a restaurant host instead of a guest, but the manager was obviously happy and unthreatened by this small man with a big smile and a hard, warm handshake.

As Connie observed him hunkering down beside a table full of young folks, she wondered how he and Maury Donovan had gotten teamed up. Was it a temporary situation? Had Phil not learned yet what an impossibly negative person Mr. Donovan was? Or was he trying to help Mr. Donovan? *That could be dangerous,* she thought. When he stopped at Maury Donovan's table, he began cleaning up the mess his own boys had made as he said, "You're a good man, Donovan, to let my sons worry you like this."

"Oh, never mind, Phil. I can take it for a few minutes. You have 'em all the time. No offense, guys," he finished, winking at his little friends.

"Tell him, Mr. Donovan. Tell Daddy about your jumping. And tell him what else you said."

"Uh-oh, I smell a big question coming," said Reverend Stone, leaning closer.

"It's just that next Saturday I'm going to be in a formation sky dive down in Gainesville and I wondered if you and Margie and the boys would like to come watch."

"Now that's an interesting offer." Phil Stone carefully piled little butter wrappers in the middle of the table and wiped his hands on a napkin, rubbing them extra long.

"Can't we, Daddy? Please?"

"You haven't been jumping lately, have you, Maury?"

"No. Wind's not been favorable. Besides, it's very difficult to get a formation team all set up. Why? You afraid I've gotten rusty?"

"No. Not that. I just hadn't heard much about your sky diving lately. Wondered if you'd quit."

"You hoped I had?" Was there an edge of irritation in

Maury Donovan's voice?

Connie looked at Mrs. Haburn, and they both spoke at once on separate subjects, then laughed at themselves, knowing they were trying not to listen to the preacher's conversation. Connie welcomed the interruption of a young woman named Jean who left her table with other young people to sit down and make friends with her. But she only half listened to Jean's comments on why she wanted to be a forest ranger.

Maury Donovan was a sky diver? What else? And why, if children loved him so much, couldn't he be a shade more lenient? She could hear his answer to that one. He wanted them to be good readers. Beginning, middle, end. And he believed he had all the answers for achieving that. The arrogant man!

four

Connie managed to get the very back seat riding home and didn't know how the trip to Toccoa Falls was concocted, didn't even realize they were headed toward Toccoa instead of Hollywood until the van turned at the entrance to Toccoa Falls College. She'd been chatting merrily with Jean about their families and about Georgia's parks. Now they wound along quiet college streets, arriving finally at a beautiful stone structure beside the Falls Trail entrance.

"There's where we should have had dinner," said Dave Olds, "at the Gate Cottage Restaurant."

"We'll do that next time," responded Phil cheerily. "There's no end to the possibilities around here."

"This place looks too fancy," said Mrs. Haburn as Maury Donovan helped her alight. "I think that barbecue'd be hard to beat."

"Well, I guess we could be kidnapped real easy," said Jean as she and Connie finally crawled out of their back seat and looked around. "I had no idea we were coming here, but I'm glad we did. I love this place. Have you ever been, Connie?"

"No. My family used to vacation up here a lot. In the Georgia mountains, I mean. But usually we went to Helen and up that direction more. I don't remember this. It is wonderful, all these tall, thick trees and the rocky stream.

And we can't be far from town."

"And do you hear the waterfall? Do you *see* it? Look above the trees! This is the highest waterfall east of the Mississippi. Not the widest, or the one with the most water running over, but the highest. It is really something."

Connie caught her breath and clasped her hands tightly together as she approached the foot of the waterfall. She felt fine spray misting her face as she watched rainbows at the fall's base. Shielding her eyes, she looked far, far up where rushing liquid thunder spilled over a sheer precipice. It was almost as if it were gushing right from the sun-whitened sky.

Great rocks, like a giant's toys, lay tossed about in the foaming stream. One young couple had climbed atop a huge boulder, and Mr. Donovan was taking their picture with the waterfall in the background. Margie Stone pulled off her shoes and squealed at the shock of cold water as she waded in the edge of the stream.

Her boys, Sunday pants rolled to their knees, clambered over the giant's toy rocks all the way to the other side of what some would call a wide creek. Margie screamed for them to start back, but couldn't make herself heard above the roar. They were climbing toward the top of the fallswaterfall as their mother looked about for her husband. Phil Stone had walked with Mrs. Haburn, and the two of them were far back down the path, sitting on a bench.

Connie began to pull off her shoes to go after the boys when Mr. Donovan dashed past her, taking the stream in only three great leaps. Soon he returned with one squealing and kicking boy under each arm.

She could hear Mr. Donovan's voice above the roar, admonishing the boys as he pointed to the top of the waterfall. "That's one hundred eighty-six feet up, and when you fall from that high, there's nothing left but a broken body."

"Is that what happens if your parachute won't work, Mr. Maury?"

Maury Donovan playfully bumped the two boys' heads together and shrugged as he thrust them at their mother.

Connie turned her attention quickly to the waterfall so she wouldn't meet Maury Donovan's eyes as he turned away from the boys. The rushing water, playful in the sunshine, was flanked on each side by dark hemlocks and by hardwoods brightening with autumn color. Its beauty was shadowed by a fearsome dignity that filled her with a deep sense of awe. She would not admit to herself that she felt a considerable fascination for this big mountain of a man, too. No, she would not admit that even in her most private thoughts.

She didn't want to leave and was, in fact, one of the last to turn away from the waterfall and head back along the creek-side trail to the parking lot. She planned right then to come again with her camera, though she knew she'd be disappointed in her pictures. She would never be able to capture the majesty of the scene. Even after she followed the others, she kept turning back to look once more at the magnificent waterfall that seemed to her like a living thing.

She stopped to read a prominent historical plaque. In November 1977, thirty-nine people had been killed when

the dam above the waterfall burst and dumped Kelly
Barnes Lake on Toccoa Falls College, a four-year Christian college. Today the college was still there, stronger
than ever, with many newly built dwellings and many
stories of bravery and faith.

"It was one of the saddest, most freakish accidents
that's ever happened around here," remarked a deep voice
at her elbow.

She started visibly, totally unprepared for the height
and breadth of Maury Donovan sidling up beside her
like a little boy with his hands in his pockets.

"It was terrible," she agreed. "I can't help thinking
how awful it must have been for parents of those students, not knowing for perhaps hours whether their children and grandchildren were alive or not."

"I was young when it happened. My parents brought
me with them to help clean up one day. It was truly, to
use a trite expression, awesome. The house we worked
on had been totally ruined. It was the home of the school's
dean, I think."

"Was any of the family rescued?"

"Yes. Miraculously, all of them were. The parents and
two children were separated when the bank of water hit.
The father and his little daughter were slammed out of
the house, into the rushing torrent. His wife and son were
trapped inside where they scrambled up on top of some
cabinets, with only their chins above water. They said it
was an eternity during which each pair thought the others were in heaven. When they found each other, they
were full of praise to God."

"But what about the thirty-nine who weren't rescued?

They were Christians, too, weren't they?"

"Yes. That part's harder to explain. I guess we shouldn't even try. One of God's mysteries. Actually, you know, the families of those who had lost someone in the flood were praising God, too. I didn't really understand it, and later on I understood it even less."

Connie looked up at him, surprised at a note of bitterness that had crept into his voice.

They walked now along the Falls Trail, following the quietly chattering stream. It was such an innocent creek today. But behind them the roar of the waterfall was a reminder of how powerful water can become when gathered together.

"You mentioned your parents. Do they live near here?"

"My mother does."

"Your. . .father?"

"He's deceased."

The two little words fell like stones, no, like heavy rocks. She looked up at him, expecting an explanation. But he'd turned his head and was watching the flowing water.

She cleared her throat and wondered what to say. School, of course. Their only common ground. No, not school. Anything but that.

"What does it feel like to sky dive? I've never known a sky diver before."

Her question took a moment to drive from his face a look of rare vulnerability. But quickly the pain or fear vanished like a shadow, leaving the same self-assured blue gaze she was used to. "How does it feel just before, during, or afterward?"

"Any of the above. I don't know." She walked quickly to keep in step with his long strides.

"When I'm heading up into the sky, my equipment all ready, my heart starts thudding like the airplane's engine and I'm scared to death. When I stand in the lineup and know my turn is coming up, I have a bitter taste in my mouth and I wonder why I'm doing this one more time. Then as I float down under the parachute, I'm at total peace. Nothing matters at that moment. Not even the harsh mysteries. It's like being a baby again with no cares at all, yet having adult sensitivity to beauty and exhilaration as the world comes up to meet me. Afterward? Well, I feel cleaned out for a while, with an afterglow of freedom. Then the gnawing begins again. Wanting to do it all over."

"Wow! Sounds like a consuming hobby."

"It used to be my career, Miss Jensen. I'm sure you've heard I was a pilot in the air force. I was still in the reserves during Desert Storm. I guess I can't get it all out of my blood."

"But now you're a principal and a minister of music and I don't know what all else. I guess you can do most anything you want to."

"Do I hear a hint of disapproval? As if you think I'm only an actor or something?"

"We're all just actors, aren't we? Didn't Shakespeare say that? But I was only wishing—"

"Yes, Miss Jensen?" They were nearing the rest of the group, and Maury Donovan paused to look down at her, startled, not for the first time, by her beauty. "What were you wishing?"

"That the Mr. Donovan I see right now would be in his office tomorrow when school opens."

One dark eyebrow lifted. His jaw firmed, his shoulders straightened. "And of course I will be. Or are you implying I'm not the same person on Sunday as on Monday?"

"I'm just thinking about little Billy Ray and how much he needs to do things that are fun to help him learn, things like beating rhythms on an old milk jug, drawing pictures no matter how black, whatever can help him get rid of some of his anger."

"Miss Jensen, don't you ever take a day off? As your principal, I definitely do recommend it." His tone was light, but edged with seriousness. He was ignoring her off-the-cuff plea for Billy Ray.

She put her hands on her hips. Sunlight caught blue-black gleams in her smooth hair that brushed softly rounded cheeks flushed pink. She was about to be too bold and she knew it, but she couldn't stop herself.

"You know, Mr. Donovan? You'd do well to use your Sunday personality all week."

"You *are* saying I'm a hypocrite. Well, you're right. Sure. So is everyone else. Lord loves us, even so, I reckon."

She couldn't argue with that. But she longed to chip this big rock of a man somehow, to make the real man step out from behind all his masks. The true Maury Donovan, she had a feeling, would let her try many methods to reach Billy Ray.

"Come on, Mr. Donovan, I want to sit next you. Come on!" yelled the littlest Stone, grabbing his big hand.

He looked back at her with an odd look of regret, she thought. She took a deep breath and followed.

≈

When the van deposited them at the church, Connie and Mrs. Haburn rode straight home, Mrs. Haburn talking nonstop about how she'd never told Connie a lie, she'd just never mentioned anything about who the minister of music was, and anyway he really wasn't all that bad. Look, how the children loved him and wasn't the waterfall wonderful and didn't she just love the Stones? Connie nodded at the right places and laughed appropriately, but her mind was not focused on what Mrs. Haburn said.

After she phoned Henry, she picked up the yellow cat and ambled down to the dock where she watched their reflections, threw in bits of stick, and chewed on a green reed. Finally, she felt better. She couldn't say why because she didn't know what had bothered her in the first place. Was it Maury Donovan's bullheadedness? Or his fleeting look of wistfulness, or despair, when he'd spoken of his father? Or was the real disturbance that she'd spent even one minute worrying about Mr. Donovan, one way or the other?

"I can't see for the life of me how a person as utterly distasteful as that man could have such nice qualities," she said to the cat, smiling as the cat's ears flicked with the movement of her breath across them.

five

In the following weeks Connie avoided Mr. Donovan as much as possible, making sure she was never the first or last one at a teachers' meeting. She attended church with Mrs. Haburn, but made sure they had their own lunch plans. Mrs. Haburn was so glad Connie would go to church with her that she didn't make much complaint, especially when Connie joined a Sunday school class and even helped Jean give a shower for a bride-to-be. Mrs. Haburn seemed content that her boarder had made friends with those "her own age" so all was well.

Connie had not given up on wanting to teach her own way. But she decided to go along with Zena and do everything possible to keep from causing unnecessary friction at school. It seemed sort of dishonest, but maybe the other teachers were right to agree with Mr. Donovan, then quietly do their own thing to a degree. It was all for a good motive, she reminded herself, to teach these children to read, write, and do their arithmetic. She thought the less she saw of Mr. Donovan, the better, all the way around.

But she hadn't reckoned with Billy Ray.

She'd read with horror of the growing number of children across the country, appearing at school with weapons. But that was in places like New York, New Orleans, and Los Angeles. Never would anything like that happen in a rural Georgia setting.

One gorgeous blue October day, finding Billy Ray wrapped in sullen anger, she told him to draw a picture of what had upset him. She returned to her desk feeling very good. Every teacher needed to practice psychiatry, she thought as she prepared to work with a reading group.

Suddenly there was a slight movement at her elbow. She turned and gasped.

"Billy Ray! Where did you get that knife?"

"It's mine. My pa gave it to me."

"Close it and hand it to me. Now." Her voice was steady. She was sure it was.

The young boy before her didn't move one of his blond hairs, and his blue eyes held hers without a blink. The pocket knife he grasped in his right hand at a menacing angle was no more than a foot away. Could she be fast enough to grab his wrists before he slashed her? If she failed, the knife could split her face or gouge her chest. Her brain went wooden, her hands sawdust. She remembered the many times Billy Ray and other boys had been pulled apart on the playground as he'd attacked them for some slur on his family. He was fast, and he'd never shown any compassion.

"Billy Ray, what is the problem? Why are you doing this?"

"Because I want to. And you can't stop me. No one can touch me or they'll be in trouble, big trouble. You can't make me do nothin' I don't want to do." Connie had never seen so much hate in one place as she saw staring from this eight-year-old boy's eyes. A fleeting vision of those eyes gleaming through prison bars made her shiver.

"The trouble will be toward you, Billy Ray. You cannot get away with this. If you'll just lay the knife down this very minute, I'll talk to your parents and try to work something out so you don't have too bad a time. But if you don't, I can't promise—"

"Your promises ain't worth a thing. Ain't no one alive keeps a promise. Richard, tie her up. Here." Billy Ray reached with one hand to pull a rope from his pocket.

Connie grabbed for Billy Ray's wrist, but missed. The knife came at her with terrifying force, but she lunged backward in her desk chair, slamming against the blackboard, her hands crossed over her face. She heard Marie scream, "Don't hurt her, Billy Ray!"

At that moment the door flew open and Zena stood there, one hand clapped to her mouth, the other one pointing to Billy Ray, who held the knife over Connie like an ice pick.

"Call for help," said Connie as calmly as she could. She realized all the other children had retreated to the back of the room near the playground exit and were huddled together, their little white faces splotched with dark eyes of fear. All were at the door except Rob, who stood in the middle of the room with both fists clenched and his eternal blank stare fixed on some high point on the blackboard.

"Call for help," Connie said again as Billy Ray nonchalantly began wiping his knife across his jeans and folding it together.

"Help!" said Zena in a whisper, her face as white as cottage cheese.

Connie, having secured the knife by now, as well as having gotten a grip on Billy Ray's shoulders, steered his body with amazing ease toward the door.

"Never mind, Zena. I'll go for help. Please stay with my children or get someone else to. I'll be back soon, class. Please, everyone, sit at your own desk. Rob. . . Joyce, see if you can help Rob, will you?"

She knew it was only because Billy Ray had recognized he was cornered that he was following her direction. Halfway down the hallway he might bolt away from her, but she really didn't know what else to do. He'd given his whole violent act up when Zena opened the door. How might it be another time?

Connie tried to ignore her own thundering heart. She had to be calm, she just had to be. No matter how bad this looked, how bad it really was, she was positive they must not send Billy Ray away. She knew she couldn't lie for the child, but could she convince Mr. Donovan to give the boy a second chance? She had to. She just couldn't give up on Billy Ray now. If they sent him away, it would be like agreeing with him that yes, Billy Ray, you really are a very bad boy. And that's all he would ever be.

Mr. Donovan, as usual, was on the telephone, but something in the faces of teacher and student arrested his attention and he did not delay in getting off the phone.

"What's the problem?" he asked, looking at Connie who continued to keep a hand on Billy Ray's shoulder and shook her head when a chair was offered her.

"Billy Ray needs to spend the rest of the day with you, I think, Mr. Donovan. Here's the knife with which he

threatened me. I think he had no idea how serious it was."
Connie imagined she must sound pretty shaky. Her tongue
was so numb and her lips so dry that she was having a
hard time speaking.

" 'Course I knowed. I ain't no dummy." Billy Ray's
face was smudged with dirt and it made his scowl even
darker.

Mr. Donovan's voice was like a coarse rasp. "Am I to
understand this child threatened you with an open knife,
Miss Jensen?" Seeing her nod he continued, "Was there
a witness other than the children?"

"Well, Miss Zena Furr heard my children scream and
came. When Billy Ray saw her, he started folding his
knife up. He did not hurt me."

Mr. Donovan looked hard right into her eyes, then
squeezed her arms, ending with a lame pat as his hands
fell away. "I'm glad you aren't hurt," he said simply.

He dropped to one knee and placed big firm hands on
the boy's shoulders. "Billy Ray, you and I will have to
talk. You stay with me now."

He looked up at Connie with a gray look around his
mouth. "Go on back to your room and reassure your children. I'll take care of this. And I'll talk to you later."

"But I—"

"We don't need you anymore, Miss Jensen. You may
go."

Just when she thought he was so human, so kind, he
started yelling at her! She didn't know what she should
have done for Billy Ray, but she knew she'd failed him
somehow. As she walked back down the hallway, she
wondered if it would have helped for her to have spent

more time with the child, given him a stump to hammer nails into. That had helped some children. Would she ever have a chance to help Billy Ray now? Her throat ached with the need for tears. But she couldn't cry now. There were the other children.

"Oh, I'm glad to see you whole and unscratched. That child is a terror, isn't he?" Zena had stood up when Connie walked in. The children were as quiet as hunched-over statues. Even Rob was at his desk.

"Don't say that, Miss Furr! He's just—a disturbed little boy. We're all fine. Or we will be once we talk about this. Richard, are you okay?"

The rope was on her desk where Richard had dropped it when Zena had opened the door. Now Connie perched herself on a cleared spot next to it. "Come here, Richard. I need to see you're all right," she said. Was she wrong not to have told Mr. Donovan that Richard had been slightly involved also? The boy was so innocent and so sweet, she wanted to take him in her arms and cuddle him like a baby left too long crying. But of course she knew better than that.

The child didn't come at first. She didn't press him. Instead she talked in a normal voice to all of her students, allowing them to ask questions as they were ready. But she kept the dark-eyed little boy, his breathing quick and shallow, in her peripheral vision. Finally, when he thought she didn't notice, he slid from his seat and crept toward her. She wasn't sure what he would do until she felt his clammy hand pat her arm. She slid off the desk and enveloped him in her arms and heard the whole class shift in their seats. Soon they were all surrounding her and tears crept down her cheeks. All this time Zena had stood near the door silently watching. Now she winked and quietly slipped out.

☙

The day lasted an eternity. When her class went to lunch, Connie saw Billy Ray sitting with Mr. Donovan in a corner of the cafeteria. *You'd have thought they were just having a cozy chat.* But she knew better. The sadness in her stomach took away her appetite completely, even though there were chicken nuggets, one of her favorite lunches.

Mrs. Gurdy had brought a container of some kind of cooked greens and a bottle of pepper sauce. She, in her wide hat, went about giving some to each teacher. Connie was glad there wasn't much left when Mrs. Gurdy reached her. Mrs. Gurdy patted her shoulder as she started to leave.

"Miss Jensen, you needn't spend any precious time worryin' about that mean little Spence boy. Why, he'll be sent off to Alpine Unit in Demorest so quick you won't even know it. I'm surprised he hadn't already been taken after he stole my billfold last year." The last sentence she whispered loudly into Connie's ear, then looked apprehensively at Richard eating at the other end of the table.

"Thanks, Mrs. Gurdy," mumbled Connie. Anything to get the woman to leave. Connie looked around at her children, some of whom had heard every word Mrs. Gurdy said, though Richard seemed totally occupied with crumbling bread into his dessert. How could she save these children from insecurity and fear?

As soon as school was out, Connie rushed straight to Mr. Donovan's office to see what he'd decided to do about Billy Ray. She was surprised to learn he had let Billy Ray go home on the bus.

He raked a hand through his thick hair and sheepishly cast his gaze toward the toes of his tennis shoes. "Against my better judgment. But I'm going up there in a few minutes. I told him I'd be there before or soon after his bus arrives. You know, he's more excited about my coming to see him than he is afraid of what I may say. Kind of humbling, isn't it?"

"He's. . .he's starved for love, I think."

"Funny you can say that after what you've been through. Are you really all right?"

"Oh, yes, I'm fine." He peered down at her with such a look of concern that she felt her cheeks go warm. "I'm fine," she repeated as he scowled and took a few paces back and forth.

"What about Richard Spence? These children stick together."

She'd been afraid he'd ask. She'd decided she was right not to bring the subject up, but now. . . . Richard couldn't help what had happened!

"Miss Jensen! Don't try hiding anything from me. I have to know everything."

"Yes. I know. Richard didn't do anything at all. . .until Billy Ray called out to him. And then he came very slowly and. . .took the rope Billy Ray told him to tie me up with. But just then is when Zena popped in. Richard is scared out of his wits. Mr. Donovan, he let me hug him after I talked to him a while.

"Oh, don't scowl. I know hugging is against the rules. But I *had* to! This was severe circumstances. Anyway, when I hugged him, it was as if I could feel every nerve in his little body quivering." Even now talking about it her eyes moistened. "You. . .we won't have to do anything to him, will we? He only did what Billy Ray said to do. He had to."

"Yes. But what might Billy Ray tell him next time? But. . .no, I hope we won't have to do anything, but you know it isn't entirely up to us. I've talked to Mr. Miles, county superintendent, and I'm to get back in touch with him after my visit to Billy Ray's this afternoon. A lot depends on the attitude of the parents, you know. Billy Ray's and Richard's."

"Have you ever talked to them before?"

"Yes. And only about trouble. With Billy Ray's brother, Lavon, and with Billy. You see, Miss Jensen—"

"You can't send Billy Ray away, Mr. Donovan. I can manage him, I know I can."

"Miss Jensen, again, it isn't our place to decide. That should be a comfort to you, that *you're* not sending him away. He got into some trouble last year and would have been placed in a special class in Demorest this fall, but there wasn't room. He's on a waiting list. But this episode will change things, I'm sure. They'll make room somehow."

"Please, Mr. Donovan, can't you do something to keep him here?"

"Well, I'm going to talk to the parents. If they could really convince us they'll make a difference in their care and control of Billy Ray, then. . . . I hate looking like trouble. That's how it will be when they see me coming. These parents, and many more, too, don't come to PTA meetings so I never see them until there's something wrong. I really do wish we could make home visits when things are okay. Then these times wouldn't be quite so bad. But there's no way we could. There's no time for the personal touches. Yes, they'll know there's trouble when they see me coming."

Connie watched her principal's face sadden as he talked, and a seed of admiration took root. "I would really like to go with you to see the children."

"I don't think that's wise, Miss Jensen."

"I don't care whether it's wise! It's the personal touch you're talking about. I need to go. I need to go for myself if not for Billy Ray. I feel like. . .I know I've let him down."

"No! Not you. Of all people, you have not let him down."

Connie was astonished at the certainty in his voice after all his belligerence and criticism.

"You have not let the boy down, Miss Jensen. And you really don't need to be exposed to any more trauma today. Look, if you need a ride home, I'll get someone to take you or at least ride along with you. I know you must be shaken up."

"Yes, I'm shaken up. But the only thing that's going to make me feel better is to let Billy Ray know that what he did has not made me hate him. Please, Mr. Donovan. Let me go with you."

He turned and walked around his desk to stare out the window, his hands in his pockets. She thought of him as he was that Sunday at Toccoa Falls with his hands in his pockets, only then so much more relaxed. He'd reminded her that day of a little boy. Now he was a man full of tension. Irrelevantly, she noticed he hadn't had his hair cut lately and it was curling above his wilted collar.

As he whirled toward his desk, snatching up the phone, his mouth set in a hard line. "I'll call the sheriff and have a car accompany us, just to be on the safe side. I'll be a few minutes making arrangements if you want to finish up in your room."

She smiled brightly as she left his office, her steps suddenly much lighter.

six

Connie squirmed in the passenger seat of Mr. Donovan's blue pickup. If only the man would chitchat, maybe they could both relax a little, but she'd run down a lengthy list of starters, getting nowhere, and now hasty glances showed that her principal's jaw had hardened. Staring straight ahead, he whipped around mountain curves. How much farther could it possibly be and still be in their school district?

They arrived at Richard's house, a small building bulging with children, and talked to his mother, who stood, arms akimbo, in the doorway and never invited them in. The pudgy woman vacillated between fear and defiance, but did give reasonable assurance that Richard would not be playing or associating with Billy Ray and that she'd watch him closely.

Turning away from Richard's home, Mr. Donovan skillfully steered the car over winding gravel roads until they finally turned onto a steep, red clay driveway that was little better than a gully. On top of a sharp knoll was a dilapidated, single-wide trailer surrounded by a collection of vehicles in various stages of deterioration. A curtain moved at one splattered window as they parked under a vast oak tree, the place's only redeeming feature.

"They're here," Connie reported.

Mr. Donovan only grunted as he slid from under the wheel. But as they approached the door, which appeared to have been bashed in several times, he put a supportive hand under her left elbow and whispered, "Let me do the talking." For once, she didn't want to argue.

Trisha Spence had squinty eyes set in a splotched face ruled by a long irregular nose. Her hair was dark, but it was hard to tell whether it was black or brown, it was so laden with grease. The lighting in her cramped living room was extremely poor, but Connie couldn't help observing a plate with a half-eaten, moldy hot dog atop a TV, dirty clothes strewn on the floor, a roach boldly crawling over food debris on the kitchen counter. Her stomach lurched.

There was no place to sit even if Trisha Spence had invited them to—and she most decidedly had not. Clad in a faded, oversized shirt and tight pants, she folded her arms across her chest and stared deadpan while Mr. Donovan explained their reason for being there.

"I don't know nothin' 'bout that," replied Trisha concerning Billy Ray's use of a pocket knife.

"Is Billy Ray here yet?"

"Naw. Bus ain't come yet."

"Mrs. Spence, I can't say too much about how serious this is. We can't jeopardize our teachers and children by allowing someone like Billy Ray to carry dangerous weapons."

"It were only a knife. Just a knife. Every kid has to have a knife."

"Not if he threatens his teacher with it. Are you listening to me? We could be in the hospital right now with

Connie Jensen bleeding from lacerations to her face and arms, and you stand there staring somewhere behind me at nothing. Where is your husband?"

Caught off guard by the question, Trisha Spence let her eyes cut ever so slightly to her right, though her head never moved. Swallowing, she repeated as if she were a robot, "Mr. Spence is delivering wood today, other side Clayton and won't be back until late. I'll tell him all about it."

"That's not good enough."

"What do you want me to do then? Billy Ray will get his whippin' if that's what you want!" For the first time, a splash of pinkness spread across her face, and she bit a swollen lip as if dealing with some remorse.

Connie stepped to her side. "That's not necessarily going to do any good with Billy Ray, Mrs. Spence. He doesn't mind pain in the least, I think. Not physical pain. I brought some of Billy Ray's pictures. I think I know a little of what's bothering him if you'd let me show you."

"I ain't got no time for such as that. We work hard to send our young 'uns to school, and from there they got to make it on their own. There, he be comin' now. Don't look like nothin's botherin' him."

Connie was close enough to hear Trisha's sigh of relief.

Billy Ray came bouncing in, red cheeked, eyes sparkling. "Hi, Mr. Donovan! Hi, Miss Jensen! You came. You really came! Want to see my chicken? I got me a chicken cooped up. He's real smart. I'm teachin' him how to count to four by peckin'." Could this merry child possibly be the same one who'd threatened Connie that very morning?

Trisha Spence grabbed the boy by both arms and shook him violently. "Hush that foolishness now an' pay attention like you've been taught. When your pa gets holt to ye, I recken you'll listen up then. What d'ya mean, showin' that knife to yer teacher like you thought a hurtin' her? Ain't you got no sense? But o' course not. You're sorry like yer brothers, not a sound, thoughty one among you. Might as well to be saddled with a pack o' wolf pups. Now you turn aroun' an' 'pologize to this pretty lady. Right now."

Having delivered this lengthy speech, the woman stepped back, replaced her arms across her chest, sealed her lips, and stared at the three awkward people before her.

Connie's arms hung limply, Billy Ray stared up at her in a mixture of defiance and ignorance, and Mr. Donovan towered over them all, his dark brows meeting.

"Sorry to scare you, Miss Jensen. It were only a joke," said Billy Ray, donning an angelic smile.

"Thank you, Billy Ray, but—"

"Son, this is not a little matter like passing a note or running in the hall. This involves safety to other people as well as yourself." Mr. Donovan had knelt as he talked so he'd be on eye level with the boy.

"Don't call him son. You ain't our father," said the older boy, Lavon, who had slid in behind them. Connie felt something against her and, looking down, stared right into the grimy, pixie face of the boys' kindergarten-age sister. The little girl smiled and took her hand. Connie wasn't sure if the child were trying to protect this strange woman who'd come to her house or if maybe she were seeking protection herself.

"You folks could be in a great deal of trouble here, and it would be smart of you not to pick on little phrases you don't like."

Mr. Donovan was losing his patience. He stood up and stared down at Billy Ray, whose blue eyes were unblinking. How did he do that, stare so hard without blinking?

"Mrs. Spence, I'll be in touch. You can send Billy Ray to school tomorrow, but someone will search him and there'd better not be anything harmful on him. He's under review for a school change already, and any more signs of rebellion can only make matters worse."

"He won't do nothin' like that again. His pa'll probably half kill him tonight."

"But, Mrs. Spence, you don't understand—" Connie began, but Mr. Donovan placed a very firm hand on her arm and shook his head.

"We'll be going now," said Mr. Donovan.

"You know there's a sheriff's car down by our road?" asked Billy Ray chattily, following them away from the door. "I'll probably be a deputy sometime. Reckon I could get a ride in that car?"

"I wouldn't try it right now, Billy Ray," said Mr. Donovan. "I had that car sent in case there was any trouble here we couldn't handle. Make sure we don't need to call them again, understand?"

"Yes, sir. But wow! Right here by my road. Pretty car. Say, you were gonna look at my chicken, weren't ya?"

It was while they were walking back around the trailer

often peering in at Billy Ray's white chicken that they saw the face of Mr. Spence at a back window. Mr. Donovan did not break his stride in the least, and Connie didn't know until they were in the truck whether he'd even noticed.

"Yes, I saw him. I knew already he was there, but I'd decided not to push it today. I have a tendency to tackle a week's work in one day, but I thought better of it this time."

"So Mr. Spence is a week's work?"

"He sure is. Say, I'm starved all the way to my backbone. We're not far from Lakeside Restaurant on Tallulah Lake and I think they'd be serving dinner by now. Go with me?"

"Well, . . .sure. Not dinner, thank you. Mrs. Haburn always cooks. But I could handle a cup of coffee about now."

"I thought so. You look a little like death on a cracker, you know."

"Thanks very much."

"No offense. Anyone would after seeing all that horror. Makes me want to choke someone when I see children having to cope with such filth and disrespect, probably downright abuse. It keeps going on, too. They'll grow up and have children who will live the same way. Unless you and I break the pattern."

Connie looked at him quickly, then broke into a genuine friendly smile. "You think there's hope for Billy Ray, don't you?"

"I'm going to do my best."

&

Mr. Donovan took the scenic gorge loop and stopped at the old overlook building on their way to the restaurant. Since the new road had bypassed this overlook, businesses had shriveled, and the long, cliff-side building was ghostly with shrill gusts of wind rattling its boarded windows. Connie stood with Mr. Donovan at the vine-grown guardrail, awed by the depth and character of the gorge as they talked about rock strata, the hardy little trees growing up the sheer gorge wall, and the distance from one craggy cliff to the other.

"It never looked any farther to anyone, I guess, than it did the day Wallenda, the Italian tightrope walker, crossed it."

"You saw him do that?"

"Well, not exactly. My parents were here and my mother was pregnant with me at the time. It was 1970. Everybody was here, they said. His cable was 1,100 feet long and the rock-studded river flowed 2,000 feet below, as it does today. That is, what's left of the river after being dammed into lakes Tallulah, Rabun, Burton, and Seed."

"I can't believe they actually saw him. I don't think I could look even if I were present for something like that." She laughed self-consciously. "Even circus tightrope walkers scare me."

He turned toward her, the wind whipping his black hair about his eyes, his collar askew. "You would have looked if you'd been here," he said. "Mother said the man was like a magnet, drawing everyone's absolute attention. It was as if they might make him fall by not looking hard enough. Spectators tried to hold their breath as if that would help him, but of course they couldn't. It took a very long, tedious time. But he made it all the way and came back. Then fell to his death some place else, Italy was it?"

"Where did he walk across the gorge?" asked Connie.

"Down river a ways. Between here and the power plant. You can still see where the cable was attached. Maybe I can show you sometime. Right now I need that food."

As Mr. Donovan ate a heaping platter of fried catfish, french fries, salad, and hush puppies, Connie sipped coffee, enjoying the view. Afternoon sun danced on Tallulah Lake and twinkled off windshields as dozens of cars traveled the new four-lane bridge. The two talked very little, but somehow Connie didn't feel threatened or uncomfortable. She was convinced Mr. Donovan really wanted the best for Billy Ray, and it changed her attitude toward the man.

When they left the restaurant, Mr. Donovan turned south, but he'd barely gotten straight in the road before he turned left into a gift shop parking lot.

"Something wrong?" Connie asked.

"No. Something I want to show you."

Before she knew it, Mr. Donovan had given her a gentle push and they were on their way along a winding nature path out to an open promontory. The gorge yawned before them, compelling their respect and admiration. Hemlock and pine mixed with autumn reds grew up the canyon walls. Down in the blue-gray distance, a thin splash of water drew itself down the rocky riverbed like the silver path of a paintbrush held in the unsteady hand of a small child. There were blobs of pools and squiggles of rapids and violent turns, but it was all so faraway Connie had to wonder if it was really water when she couldn't hear it. Mr. Donovan said there were several falls down there, yet she wasn't ever positive that the roar she heard was water and not the wind.

"It's like seeing a different side of someone's face," he said to explain their need to see this view, also.

But her thoughts had reverted to Billy Ray.

"I know what I could do!" she exclaimed, turning toward him, her brown eyes sparkling. "I could teach Billy Ray separately for a while. In-house suspension, you know? Maybe the review committee would let us continue if it worked out. Please, would you let me try?"

Connie was encouraged that he didn't immediately pick her up and throw her over the cliff. But she saw storm clouds gathering in his rugged face. "Where would you do this?"

"Why. . .I guess in your office. Wouldn't that be the best place?"

He grinned. "Not if you wanted to use your haphazard approach to teaching, Miss Jensen."

She blushed. Haphazard! So that's what he thought! It seemed a good thing just then to sit down on a convenient bench and become very occupied with studying the other side of the gorge. Was that hemlock growing right out of a rock? It certainly looked like it.

He sat down beside her. "So what kind of methods would you use? To teach Billy Ray, I mean? After all, you'd still have your whole classroom, and you can't be two places at once."

Thankful he was at least talking about it, she plunged into sharing some of her ideas. With Billy Ray, maybe she could experiment, try some of her art and music ideas and prove to Mr. Donovan how helpful they could be.

"I just can't believe that you are so against things like measuring salt to learn math or dressing up as characters and acting out a story in reading. This is the middle of the nineties and these methods have been taught in education classes since back in the dark ages, all the way back to the sixties anyway. You've told us to hold science, health, and home ec for upper grades, but don't you know the children need stepping stones to prepare for later learning? And we can *use* those subjects to teach reading and arithmetic."

When she dragged her eyes away from the gorge and looked at Mr. Donovan she was startled at the naked pain in his face. Or was it sorrow, or defeat? Something was vastly wrong for him, she knew that. She hugged herself against a chilling breeze and half whispered, "I'm sorry. I was way out of line. Should we be going now?"

"No. No, you weren't really out of line. I asked for it. And no, we can't go yet. I. . .I need to tell you something."

He was quiet so long she thought he'd forgotten what he was going to say. He dropped his head into his hands at one point as if he had a headache.

"It's all right, you know," she said not knowing what to say, but sure she must do something. "Whatever it is, you don't have to tell me, really."

That made him smile. "You're not the world's greatest psychiatrist, that's for sure."

"I think I'm pretty good," she returned, squaring her shoulders.

"Extremely modest, too," he added. His smile faded. He seemed to gather himself together for a great undertaking. "I don't know why I'm telling you this," he said finally, watching a bird circle far below as he leaned forward, elbows on knees.

"Well, if you must tell me, then get on with it," she said, laughing nervously.

He smiled at her as if she were a naughty child who had just done something nice. "Thank you. I will then."

She waited, pulled her sweater closer around her, picked up a pine cone to examine it, and waited again. When he cleared his throat and began talking, she squeezed the pine cone so hard it left marks in her hand.

"I know I'm unreasonable in allowing so little extra-curricular activity around the school. Sometimes I wonder I still have a job, and I know I wouldn't if it weren't for my mother and her politics. She watched this job like a hawk and made sure I had it as soon as I'd taught a couple of years. She knew I wanted more than anything to make sure every child in my care learns to read. And she knew what started that desire in my life.

"You see, my father couldn't read. Oh, he was the smartest man I've ever known. And no one but the two of us and my mom knew he couldn't read. Why, he even memorized a Sunday school lesson every week and taught a class! But if someone ever asked him to read anything, of course he'd always forgotten his glasses or had a piece of dust in his eye or had a sudden coughing spell. I got very angry at him once because he couldn't read, and I yelled at him that I would teach him myself.

"He did let me try. But nothing I did ever worked. He simply could not distinguish phonetic sounds. I used flash cards and tried to drill letters and words into him. Many an evening I began my own homework at eleven because of working with Dad all evening. And he hated it. Sometimes it seemed as if. . .he hated me, too. We got so frustrated with each other, my mother finally stopped it all."

Connie tried, like the Wallenda spectators, to hold her breath as Mr. Donovan crossed his own gorge full of rocky feelings. She was afraid he would turn back into his old raspy self before he told her everything. But in a low rumbling voice he continued.

"I was away at college when it happened. Dad developed pretty bad angina. He kept nitroglycerine pills ready all the time and was, as always, the life of any gathering, the muscle of any work job, and the epitome of happiness. He loved his garden better than almost anything except Mother and spent nearly all his waking hours preparing soil, planting, or harvesting.

"That's where Mother found him one day when she got home from the grocery store. He was face down in the dirt, one hand gripping tightly his nitroglycerine bottle. He was too far gone for CPR to revive him and he died on the way to the hospital. When I got there, Mother was hysterical and all she could say was 'He had his medicine. Why didn't he take it?' I looked at the bottle which she said he'd just gotten the day before. It was a new bottle with a child-safe cap and. . .well, you see, he couldn't read the directions for opening and apparently, in his pain, just could not figure it out."

Connie ached for the man beside her who was so obviously still grieving for a father dead now ten years. She couldn't say anything. To speak seemed as out of place as getting up to make an announcement in the middle of a preacher's sermon. After what seemed several minutes, she laid one slim hand on the seat beside him and without a word he laid one of his big ones over it. For long minutes they sat that way. Connie didn't consider that it was anything unusual until they stood to leave. Then she realized she missed his big warm hand.

⁂

Neither of them spoke on the return trip to Pine Ridge. Once there, she expected him to say, "See you tomorrow" or some such trite farewell and leave her to start her car alone. But he jumped out and met her at her door. Before she could fish her keys out of her bag he placed hands on her shoulders as he had done earlier that day. Then, it was to be sure she was all right after Billy Ray's threat. Now, he held her shoulders firmly as he said, "Thank you, Connie."

Then with no warning he leaned over and kissed her. She tasted the tracks of salty tears on his lips, yet his lips were so strong and so good. With a whirlwind of new feelings chasing each other through her head and her heart, she watched him walk away.

As she drove home, she touched two fingers to her lips and laid the hand he'd touched against her cheek. He was such an odd man, and there was so much more to him than she'd realized. She had seen his face from a different angle, she thought, remembering his comment about the gorge. But no matter what, she wouldn't even hint to Mrs. Haburn that she'd changed her mind one little bit concerning Maury Donovan.

When she turned in at Mrs. Haburn's and plunged down the little steep road, she had the feeling something more was going to happen before the day was over, that as full as it had been, there was still more. Mrs. Haburn was in the kitchen and announced cheerfully they'd have to go to the grocery store if company was coming for the weekend.

"But are we expecting company, Mrs. Haburn?"

"I forgot I hadn't even told you. You're so late or I would have told you long ago. Anyway, Henry called. Said he'd be here Friday evenin'. Now you don't worry about a thing, child. I'll take care of things around here and you can just relax and enjoy your friend. I've already figured out we can have chicken pie Friday night. No man alive has ever not liked my chicken pie. And Saturday lunch we can have fried chicken if you don't think that's too much chicken. An' I guess you two would be goin' out Saturday night, but if you want to eat before you go we could have country fried steak and mashed potatoes, one of my favorites. And of course roast beef on Sunday. . . ."

Connie closed her bedroom door behind her and pressed fingers against her eyes. She went to bed praying for Billy Ray and for wisdom concerning Henry. Even with her room darkened, she could still imagine the picture of the praying couple in their field and wished that when she prayed she could be as confident when she prayed as they seemed to be.

She was almost asleep when she realized Mr. Donovan had called her Connie.

seven

Henry arrived right on schedule at six o'clock Friday evening, smelling of his usual cologne and full of quiet cheer. He was genuinely happy to see Connie. She tried hard to appear glad to see him, too, though there was something very wrong about the whole thing and she knew it. They went to a movie in Toccoa after eating Mrs. Haburn's wonderful chicken pie. Henry did most of the talking going and coming and seemed satisfied with Connie's very lame comments.

Saturday morning they strolled down to the dock and she tried to explain Billy Ray to him without actually telling him about the knife. She just said Billy Ray had gotten into too many fights and was to be in some form of suspension for several weeks, that the principal was going to teach him himself from lesson plans she prepared for him. Which was all true. Mr. Donovan had made up his mind he was going to teach Billy Ray himself and for three days now that had worked out fine. But Henry didn't really hear much of what she said. He did hear her story about washing Marie's hair and how very happy the little girl was, flipping her beautiful brown hair about and feeling it as she did her work.

"Connie, you're not supposed to be washing hair. You're not a beautician, you're a teacher! What next?"

If he only knew!

After lunch they went to Clayton and rode out Warwoman Road, enjoying the autumn color splashed up the slopes of Screamer Mountain, exploring a portion of old railroad bed dating back to the Civil War, and eating a chocolate bar while passing between sweeping skirts of thick, dark hemlock in a little park. As long as there was plenty to talk about other than personal feelings, Connie could have a reasonably good time. But deep inside she felt guilty, as if she were cheating Henry.

Referring to a delightful North Georgia guidebook she'd picked up, Connie asked Henry if he'd rather go to Mark of the Potter on the Soque or go all the way to Helen, Georgia's alpine village, maybe even up the scenic Russell Highway.

"Hmmm. Doesn't really matter," said Henry. "Only let's don't go as far as Helen. I came to see you, Connie, not to sightsee. Let's find a nice place to sit and talk."

Even after that comment, Connie, who was driving, put off serious talking by jabbering about landmarks they passed, filling Henry's ears with mountain trivia in which he had no interest. They drove all the way back to Clarkesville, turned up the Lake Burton Road, had cinnamon rolls and coffee at Batesville General Store, then backtracked to the Mark of the Potter. By the time they arrived at the old gristmill made into a gift shop, the afternoon was old for Connie in more ways than one.

Connie usually liked to browse around and see all the beautiful crafts, particularly watch pottery being formed by skilled craftsmen. But quickly she realized Henry was miserable. Pottery was far from his cup of tea. That's when she suggested they go out on the deck and throw some of the provided feed in the river for the fish. Wonderful, long sleek trout frisked or hovered in the stream, and Connie giggled at the sport they made of a handful of feed.

"It's good to hear you laugh, Connie," said Henry, laying an arm across her shoulders. "I've missed your laughter, you know. I. . .I'll be so glad when you come back. Things aren't right when you're not around."

Connie tossed in the last little pellets of feed, then turned her back to the railing, lightly shedding Henry's arm. Taking a deep breath, she plunged into truthfulness.

"Henry, things are never going to be the same again. If I could make this easier I would. I've tried to think of a good way to do it. But all I know is to tell you straight out. I. . .I just can't. . .marry you, Henry."

He seemed so intent on watching the fish she thought for a minute he hadn't heard her above the roar of the water and his own concentration. But finally he turned toward her, and she was startled at the white pain in his face. "You've found someone else, I suppose."

"No. But, Henry, I don't believe I love you. Not the way I should. I care for you a whole lot. But. . .that's not good enough."

"When did you realize?"

She wouldn't have known before he asked, but now she said, "When you chided me for washing Marie's hair."

"But, Connie, I'm sorry about that. I just—"

"No, Henry, it's all right. Only. . .you see, we're so very different, and I don't think we'd be happy. I was proud of washing Marie's hair, and it thrilled me to see her feeling pretty. It was important to me. I'm sorry, Henry, but here, I better give you your ring back."

"Not here, Connie. Wait until we get to the car. You might drop it in the river. Come on. Let's go."

❧

Connie could not understand why Henry couldn't have humored poor Mrs. Haburn a bit and stayed long enough to eat her beautiful dinner. But Henry grabbed his things up from Mrs. Haburn's sewing room, which he'd slept in, and was gone in minutes.

"Something wrong with my nose?" asked Mrs. Haburn, staring at the firmly closed door. "I didn't smell nothin' wrong with that steak."

Connie laughed half-heartedly. "No, no, it wasn't the steak, Mrs. Haburn. It's I who doesn't smell so good."

Mrs. Haburn whirled so quickly she immediately began massaging her arthritic neck, but at the same time she eyed her young boarder with open curiosity. Breaking into a contagious cackle, she declared, "Well, you smell like a rose to me. And. . .is Henry gonna be callin', d'ya think?"

"No, I don't think so." Connie's eyes brimmed with sudden tears and Mrs. Haburn hugged her very tightly. She had the good sense not to mention how very glad she was that that match hadn't worked out.

❧

Connie was amazed at Mr. Donovan's determination, his persistence in teaching Billy Ray, as days and weeks went by with so little progress. For whatever reason, the review board had not yet transferred Billy Ray, and

Connie felt that Mr. Donovan had a lot to do with it. But if he didn't make some progress soon, teaching Billy Ray addition facts, spelling, and how to write. . . .

Mr. Donovan's secretary was out for the day so Connie left her class under the care of the school's roving aide for a few minutes and went to see if she could help Billy Ray. She didn't mean to eavesdrop, but paused indecisively at the door.

"Billy Ray, there are some things you just have to learn," said Mr. Donovan in a tone as if he'd said it already at least a hundred times. "Don't give me that dead-pan stare, either. I know and you know that you can do this. Come. C-O-M-E. Come. As I've told you, letters make up our code and you have to break it to communicate. I'm letting you in on the secret. Go, G-O. Come, C-O-M-E. Now you have to learn the difference or when your girlfriend writes 'Come,' you'll go instead."

"Don't never plan to have a girlfriend," grunted Billy Ray. "My pa said I don't need none of this stuff to get along. Weren't for my mama, I'd be workin' with him."

A tense silence followed. Connie gripped her hands together, wondering if she should go in or turn very quietly and leave. She jumped as something heavy crashed. Flinging the door open, she saw Mr. Donovan's face ablaze with anger and Billy Ray crouching defensively. Mr. Donovan had knocked his own chair over and now proceeded to set it back up, a sheepish look overcoming his anger.

"I ain't done nothin'," blurted Billy Ray. "You gonna put me in jail for not learnin' C-O-M-E, come?"

Connie stared at the little boy, then at Mr. Donovan's

astonished face. The two adults burst out laughing and
Billy Ray's ears turned very pink.

After that Connie was much more respectful of Mr.
Donovan and his rote method. On the other hand, Mr.
Donovan broke down and asked her advice quite a number of times, though she couldn't see that he ever used it.
She could see that he seemed less like a charging bull
these days, and that helped the school's general atmosphere.

Other teachers noticed a change in Mr. Donovan, too,
and marveled to Connie how he must have a soft spot for
tough little boys. Zena Furr even went so far as to say
she thought he had a soft spot for Connie because he let
her get away with some things he'd never allowed them
to do, like planning a musical Thanksgiving play that
required an hour of practice each day for two weeks. Or
allowing her to teach Billy Ray how to play a harmonica,
which was a huge thrill to both her and her pupil. Billy
Ray was seldom seen after that without his mysteriously
donated harmonica at his lips. Mr. Donovan said Miss
Jensen should have been in Singapore instead of teaching him to play, but there was a small twinkle in his eyes
when he said it.

But whatever Zena said, Connie couldn't feel Mr.
Donovan had a soft spot for her. Not when week after
week he spoke to her only professionally, never seemed
to recall their conversation at the gorge. In church group
meetings, his laughter seemed to quiet when she entered
the room. All she could think was he'd been awfully
sorry he kissed her and he hoped she'd forget all about
it. After all, it was only a momentary departure from

reality in the heat of overwrought nerves.

But she couldn't forget, not his firm vibrant kiss nor the warmth of his big hand protecting hers, accepting her sympathy, as they sat by Tallulah Gorge.

One day while standing in front of his desk waiting for him to get off the phone so she could explain Billy Ray's lesson plan, she idly scanned his big planning calendar flopped open right before her eyes. She didn't mean to be snooping, she just happened to see that the following Saturday was a flying day. Sky divers were scheduled to land at 2:30 P.M. at Gainesville's small airport. She didn't know exactly when she decided for sure she was going, but when she woke up that Saturday morning, there was no doubt in her mind, and she dressed with as much excitement as if it were Christmas morning.

Connie was glad she'd added an extra layer of sweat shirt under her jacket when she saw ice on the pond. Driving to Gainesville on such a clear bright morning was a pleasure even with the sound of Mrs. Haburn's cautions ringing in her ears: "Wherever you're going, drive carefully, watch for ice patches, and be very careful on bridges." Of course she didn't know where Connie was going or she would really have been full of cautions.

That morning Connie had prayed with Mrs. Haburn as usual, and it was pretty hard not to tell her landlady about her exciting adventure, but she didn't dare. Besides, there was hardly time after she related all the cases at school for which she wanted Mrs. Haburn to pray. Rob was there only half-days, yet he vandalized the other children's pencils and work when he was there. Sammy Craven was doing very well as long as she worked closely with him. He was pretty lazy, she'd decided. There was Joyce, so much brighter than most, who could read and write now, but needed high motivation.

And then there was Richard, who had become sullen since Billy Ray's absence from the classroom. Richard no longer made happy detailed pictures, but whatever his assignment, his paper was covered with ugly monsters. And, of course, she wanted Mrs. Haburn to pray for little Marie who'd learned to read and wanted a new book every day.

As Connie drove, thinking of all her prayer requests and how Mrs. Haburn took each one like a precious responsibility, she smiled to herself. To begin with, Connie had prayed with Mrs. Haburn to make her landlady happy. Now, Connie realized, she herself wanted prayer time. *Maybe this is what growing as a Christian means,* she thought. She'd always wondered about that lofty phrase, "growing as a Christian."

She shopped a little in Gainesville, had lunch, and soon afterward, headed for the airport. She wasn't sure where at the airport she should go, but soon spotted a small knot of people over to one side staring at the sky. That must be the place. She shyly stationed herself a short distance away, close enough to hear some of the others' comments, far enough away so they didn't have to feel they must talk to her.

It was so, so bright, even with sunglasses. Connie stared up into the sky, seeing nothing but clear, unclouded space entered occasionally by small planes approaching or departing. *That group of spectators has to be awfully dedicated to stick to this activity for very long,* she thought, rubbing her neck.

"Roger was wishing they could have done formations today," said one vigorous young woman with her sleeves pushed up as if it were late spring instead of early December.

"I know. Jock, too. Of course it's not the same for him since he never jumps anymore, but he loves to fly the plane. Makes him feel he's still part of the group. And he gets so excited when they do the formations. He's always so keyed up nights before that he can't sleep a wink."

The second speaker was probably about forty, Connie thought, an attractive woman wearing a hand-knit beret of bright red with matching mittens, which she was constantly removing and replacing. When she wasn't taking her mittens on or off, she was lacing her fingers or putting her hands together as in prayer.

Suddenly Connie realized the woman in the red beret was speaking to her. "Do you have someone in the sky, honey?" she asked.

"Oh, no. I mean, well, yes, I am watching someone, but he doesn't even know I'm here. It's just my school principal. I'm a teacher and I thought—"

"Of course, of course. You must work for Maury Donovan then."

"Well, yes, how did you know?"

"He's the only principal in the group, that's all," said the woman walking over to introduce herself. "I'm Jock's wife, Betty Friedman. We all like Maury Donovan. But he and my husband are especially close. They were in the service together, even though Maury's a lot younger than we are."

"I'm Connie Jensen. It's very nice to meet you. Isn't it about time they were coming down?"

"Oh, it varies, you know. They may have run into some air pockets or something and decided to fly up over the lakes before they jump. When those four get together, you can never tell what they're going to do." Betty laughed with her head thrown back, her eyes constantly scanning the skies.

Connie relieved the crick in her neck by looking around at the rest of the spectators. One man was a chain smoker. Another one cracked crude jokes, one right after another. Connie noticed Betty, though she didn't voice any complaints, simply did not even smile at the man's jokes. One very pretty woman looked old enough to be a mother to some of the jumpers. Could that be Maury's mother? She tried to see some resemblance, but couldn't, for the woman was small and blond.

"Are you ever worried, I mean really worried, about your husband when he's up there?" asked Connie of Betty Friedman.

Betty looked into her eyes briefly before turning her face back up. "Yes. I worry. It's impossible not to sometimes. But he dearly loves to do this. More than anything. And I just decided a long time ago I'd rather come and watch than sit home and worry. Everyone has to make their own adjustments to things like this. But I believe we're happier than folks who only stay home and watch all their sports on television. Oh. . .I see the plane now. That's our plane," she showed Connie, pointing a red hand, her voice shaking with excitement.

Connie had trouble seeing the plane very well, the glare was so bad, but she could hear it. "Sounds as if it's stopping," she said uneasily.

Betty laughed. "Jock's letting the jumpers out. There's one. . .two. . .three. He doesn't really stop, but it does sound like it. Now, there he goes to circle and come back down."

"But. . .where are the jumpers?"

"Can't you see them? They're only specks yet. But it won't be long before you'll hear Maury Donovan singing. He always sings when he comes down. Reminds me of that beautiful piece of music called 'On Wings of Song.'" She cut loose right that minute, humming strains of music Connie had never heard before.

"Not that Maury sings that song. I've never even heard words for it. But the way he sings so happy and free makes me think of 'On Wings of Song.' I'm not really crazy, Connie, just wacky," she said, one red-mittened hand shading her eyes from the sunshine.

Connie glanced at the woman beside her, drawn by her enthusiasm, then studied the skies again. Now she could see them! Even as she watched, funny blobs or dark specks developed into colorful umbrellas as one by one the parachutes opened. There was a cheer from the whole little earthbound audience. Then almost a reverent silence settled on them so that, sure enough, as Betty had said, they could hear Maury Donovan's rich bass belting out " 'There's a land that is fairer than day, and by faith I can see it afar. . . .' "

Connie shivered and pulled her jacket closer as she stared steadily at the descending parachutes. It was amazing how slowly they came down. She was wishing Maury Donovan would sing again so she could try to tell which one he was when Betty pulled at her arm and pointed him out.

"That one," she said urgently, "the one with the red and white canopy."

Connie was first of all astonished when the jumpers landed so neatly on their feet amid billows of colorful silk. Then she was suddenly envious as several of the women ran to embrace their men at various landing places around the airport. She noticed the little blond woman, though excited for them, did not budge from beside the chain smoker. They were just friends of the jumpers, she supposed. She watched the jumper with the red and white canopy and saw only Betty Friedman in her red beret running over to him to hug his neck.

Having decided to disappear quietly, Connie couldn't wait to get her car cranked and be away from there. She wouldn't stop long enough to tell Betty good-bye or hear all the glowing reports and, mainly, she wouldn't talk to Maury Donovan and he could think whatever he wanted to when he found out she'd been there. It had simply been a matter of good healthy curiosity, that's all. She couldn't have lived with Mrs. Haburn for three months without acquiring a huge case of inquisitiveness.

She fumbled with her keys, her fingers cold in her gloves. At the moment she finally slid key into ignition a shadow seemed to pounce on her car and she gasped out loud. The shadow turned out to be a fully suited Maury

Donovan minus his parachute, his face glowing like sunrise on Easter morning.

Having done a spread eagle across her side of the windshield, he jerked her door open and pulled her out. Very deliberately, he slid her sunglasses from her face and tossed them into her car, then enveloped her in the biggest, warmest hug she'd ever known, nestling his face in her hair and gently rocking with her for long minutes. Airport sounds—droning of a plane overhead, shouts of other happy sky divers, and flapping of a windsock—drifted about them as they clung to each other.

When Maury Donovan whispered, "Will you go with me to get a bite to eat?" Connie nodded her dark head against his cheek.

ಌ

In a friendly sandwich shop they huddled over a booth table talking about the jump. Maury's face was still glowing and his descriptions of the total peacefulness and exuberance in the ten-thousand-foot descent lit sparkles in Connie's eyes as well.

"People think our biggest thrill is in watching the earth from the air and, of course, that is a lot of fun. It's so beautiful from up there. You don't see the trash anymore, or wrecked cars, or abandoned buildings. Everything is green or brown, spiky or soft looking in fascinating squares and rectangles as pasture, fields, or forests rise to meet you. But better than what I can see is what I feel up there. I feel stripped of all encumbrances, Connie, so I can really praise the Lord. It is just incredible!"

The waitress brought his sandwich and fries and he

ate ravenously, explaining between bites that he never ate anything before a jump. "Far too excited to eat. Haven't had a bite since last night. Just some orange juice this morning."

"Mr. Donovan, you're going to need more than one sandwich, I think," said Connie softly.

He wagged a finger at her and tried to speak, but his mouth was too full. Finally what came out was, "You've got to call me Maury when we're away from school. Can't you do that?"

"Yes, of course I can. . .Maury."

"Now that's better. And, yes, I think I will have another sandwich, maybe two more. Don't you want anything?"

"No, thank you. I'm only an earthling, you know, and can't be expected to have your heavenly appetite."

He laughed with her, but in the middle of the laugh his eyes dropped suddenly to her left hand and impulsively he reached for her ring finger, rubbing the empty finger with his thumb. "I've been wanting to ask. . .what happened?" he asked.

"We. . .just. . .aren't suited for each other. I gave him his ring back long ago. In October."

"I knew it was missing, but didn't know why. Guess I was kind of bashful about finding out."

"You, Maury? Bashful?" She laughed and shook her head.

"Under every tough skin there is a boy, Connie," he said, chewing more thoughtfully now.

"Speaking of boys, you've sure made a difference for Billy Ray. Isn't he doing pretty well now?"

A cloud crossed his face. "Let's don't talk about school, Connie, please. But, since you asked, yes, the boy's doing fine. Just needs lots of attention. More than he'll ever dream of getting in that cesspool where he lives."

"Maury!"

"Well, it is. And you're the one who brought up this subject."

"Well, I'm sorry, I'll change it. Does your mother ever come to watch you jump?"

He was in the middle of a big bite, but Connie thought he took an extra long time finishing the bite before he answered. Then it was a curt, "No." Nothing more, just no.

She was baffled and would not let it drop. "Why not?"

"Because she chooses not to. That's all."

She didn't know how to respond and simply folded and refolded her napkin until he mentioned something about the wind and soon they were talking about flying again.

When they went back to the airport to get her car, the place was quiet as a school in July. The windsock wasn't even flapping, and planes tied in their places didn't look as if they'd ever be airborne again.

"Far from the circus atmosphere of a couple hours ago," commented Maury, unfolding himself from under the wheel to see her into her own car. "But then we can't stay on mountain tops or at a circus. Lord made us to have highs and lows and lots in between. I think what I need now is about seventy-two hours of sleep. But I'll see you in church tomorrow."

"With your eyes open?"

"Maybe I can prop them open with sixteenth notes," he answered, playfully pulling one eyelid up. He leaned elbows on her open window and she thought he might kiss her, but he only squeezed her shoulder with a big hand, then stood back and waved her off.

Why didn't he want to talk about his mother? she wondered, as she started home. The more she thought about it, the more indignant she became. The man had drawn too many lines. Don't talk about school, don't talk about my mother, just talk about flying, mainly just flying. Well, Zena Furr was right, Connie decided. She did need to leave Mr. Maury Donovan well alone.

eight

In spite of all her wise cautions to herself, Connie did hope very much to see Maury at church, but she didn't see him for more than a minute privately. He directed the choir in a wonderful rendition of "When I Survey the Wondrous Cross," which brought tears to her eyes. And his face was far from sleepy as he led congregational singing. She imagined he beamed right at her several times and she knew her smile gave away the fact that she liked his looks very much.

When church was out, she walked slowly beside Mrs. Haburn, who not only was hobbling worse that day, but was compelled to have a long chat with everyone she met. Suddenly Maury was beside them explaining quickly that the preacher needed him to take a carload of youth to a Bible drill meet that afternoon. "I'll see you soon," he said over his shoulder as he hurried away.

Mrs. Haburn had a bad bout with arthritis in her neck and left knee that afternoon and they decided not to get out in the evening air to go to church, though Mrs. Haburn worried that dear Reverend Stone would think she didn't want to hear his promised message on angels.

Connie didn't see Maury until Monday morning and then only to give him Billy Ray's lesson plan very hurriedly since he had put a caller on hold and her own class was waiting. She didn't think too much about it that day. It was really what she'd expected, knowing the routines of school days. But by the end of the week when he hadn't called or spoken privately to her, she began to have forebodings. She had no right to expect anything more than a friendly nod from him, yet her disappointment deepened every day. How could she have totally misread his feelings expressed in a kiss, a hand touch, and a hug?

Mrs. Haburn had baked her fruitcakes right after Thanksgiving so they'd have time to season really well before Christmas. Now, on December 13, she was ready to make fudge if, as she said, the weather would cooperate with her. And if Connie could help get her ingredients together. She needed some walnuts and she was out of vanilla. Would Connie pick those up after school?

"I'll not only pick them up for you, I'll help you crack the nuts," said Connie cheerfully as she left for school in predawn darkness. It was her week to be on bus duty.

The first sign that day that everything was going wrong was when Richard wet his pants. She was trying so very hard to teach him how to read. Why, if he could make pictures of anything he wanted to, couldn't he learn simple words like run? In chin-hard determination, she refused to let him leave her desk until he completed one whole page of reading, which was actually only six lines. When he said he needed to go, she simply restated that he must stay there until he finished. Then he wet his pants and she had to go to the school's front office to find dry clothes.

While she was in the office, Connie saw the sheriff enter Mr. Donovan's office, a hard-looking deputy with him. She didn't understand what they were there for since she was in such a hurry to see about Richard, but the news spread rapidly. Seems they'd arrested Billy Ray Saturday outside a grocery store where they found candy bars and crackers, good for which he hadn't paid, stowed in the pockets and lining of his jacket. They'd let him go with a severe reprimand and return of the goods, but this morning he'd done the same thing at a jiffy store.

"I think he's going to have to go to reform school, if they take them that young," said Zena while their children played at recess. "You know he's not safe to have around, Connie!" she remonstrated, seeing the defeated look on her friend's face.

Connie looked at little Richard, Billy Ray's cousin, sitting alone against the playground fence, and for the first time wondered if there really was any hope for either of them. Richard's parents had never offered any more support since questioning them concerning Richard's part in the knife threat, and Billy Ray's parents were totally uncooperative. If it hadn't been for Mr. Donovan, Billy Ray would have already gone to the disciplinary class in Demorest. Maybe, just maybe, he could stall the review board one more time.

But this was one time too many, the sheriff said.

Connie tried to be truthful but gentle in explaining to her children what had happened for, of course, they found out and were full of questions. Marie was the one most upset. She cried for an hour, her head down on her desk, sobbing over and over, "They'll make the dogs chase Billy Ray."

Marie wasn't consoled by anything Connie could say

whether she explained that Billy Ray wouldn't be chased, wouldn't be in jail in the first place, or that he would be back in just a few weeks for good behavior. But finally little mothering Joyce hit on a comforting thought when she said, "Marie, Billy Ray can run faster than a deer, and if those dogs do get after him, he'll leap high over a fence and be long gone."

Connie shuddered at the influence of television on her children. Most of all, she mourned losing Billy Ray. She wanted to lay her head down like little Marie and just cry, but of course she didn't have that privilege.

Mr. Donovan came to her room to report what had happened, almost as if they'd had no other communication about Billy Ray, as if he were simply the principal reporting to the teacher of a delinquent student, nothing more.

She almost forgot about walnuts and vanilla, and didn't remember until she'd slowed as usual to turn in by Mrs. Haburn's apple sign. In the nick of time, she accelerated and drove on toward Clarkesville.

She was so tired that she didn't feel like hurrying. The store was merry with Christmas supplies, and she took her time looking at all the nuts, choosing walnuts from a loosely filled barrel, collecting some navel oranges, and admiring miniature, Norfolk pine, ready-dressed Christmas trees. She and Mrs. Haburn had bought a Christmas tree the weekend before, but she wondered if Mrs. Haburn would like one of these tiny trees to put on the dining table. About then she heard someone say the name Maury and she glanced around.

Two women were standing in front of the cabbages,

catching up on the news. One was a tall spare woman with a loose-fitting coat, short iron gray hair, and bright blue eyes.

"Maury's doing fine, thank you. He's still principal at Pine Ridge."

"Any young lady friend I haven't heard about?"

"No. Maury dates, but never settles down to liking only one. I'll probably be a grandmother when I'm too old to spoil the grandchildren!"

So this spare-framed lady with iron gray hair was Maury's mother! Connie studied the Christmas trees even harder, hoping it would appear she was trying to choose the very healthiest one.

"Well, have a merry Christmas now. Tell that handsome hunk of a son hello for me. Maury's always been one of my favorites."

"Merry Christmas to you, too, Susan," said Mrs. Donovan.

Connie had found Maury's mother! Driven by either an insatiable curiosity or something even stronger, she followed the woman all through the store, up and down the aisles. She collected a half buggy full of groceries Mrs. Haburn hadn't requested, including the Norfolk pine and, in the meantime, observed subtly how Mrs. Donovan seemed sad and lonely, though some people did speak to her. She put very little in her cart, things easily prepared for only one person.

Connie longed for some chance to introduce herself to the woman, but could never think of any courteous way of bringing it about. Even if she could, what good would it do? They couldn't discuss the thing that haunted Maury so, the death of his father caused by his illiteracy.

When Connie arrived home, Mrs. Haburn was fit to be tied because Connie was so late. The bustling little woman rattled all through supper about that and other things. "We didn't need all that stuff, I just asked for walnuts and vanilla and I don't know why you got all them things. Not that we can't use 'em, mind you. You'd be surprised how quick I can get out of things. Like flour, for instance. Since you went hog wild, it's a good thing you thought to get flour because I might have been sendin' for some in a couple o' days. All the Christmas bakin', you know. I need to make cookies for your class, Connie, maybe gingerbread boys and girls. You need to tell me exactly how many of each."

And, of course, Mrs. Haburn couldn't be huffy long while that merry little Norfolk pine was smiling at her from the center of the table. Connie was glad one good thing had come out of this dreary day. If it was dreary to her, how much drearier to Billy Ray, placed in a strange foster home? She wondered what he might be doing about now, probably sulking and making his foster parents miserable. Whoever they were, they needed a *lot* of prayer! She wished she could take Billy Ray his own box of gingerbread boys. Would she be allowed to do that?

❧

The next afternoon when she dragged her bone-weary self into her room to clean up after finishing her bus duty responsibilities, Maury Donovan followed her. Without a word, he picked up a broom and went to work. She straightened up the desks, rehung a fallen poster, cleaned the blackboard, and snapped all the smudgy work sheets into her attaché case to take home and grade. The principal had sat down on a corner of her desk by then and was watching her.

"I think Billy Ray is vastly better off where he is," he said. "He's with a good family. We've had children they kept before and I've always been impressed with their care. He goes to the Alpine Unit in Demorest where they're trained to care for disturbed children. It's pretty much as usual for him except. . .well, I know his teacher's not nearly as pretty nor as talented as the one he left behind."

She was so astonished at his compliment she couldn't think of what to say. Clearing her throat, she asked, "Would it be all right if I take him some of Mrs. Haburn's cookies?"

"I think so. I'll give you the directions. The family's in Clarkesville, not hard to find."

"You've been to see him?"

"Of course. Had to get him settled in, you know. Connie—"

"Yes, sir?"

"Please don't 'Yes, sir' me right now."

"We're still at school, sir."

"Well, then, let's go somewhere."

"I don't think so. I. . .I'm very busy with all these papers to grade."

"I see. Connie, look, I know I've been unkind lately. I just want a chance to explain."

"You don't need to do that. It's totally unnecessary. Would you lock the door for me? My hands are full. Papers to grade and forms to fill out. Papers, papers, papers. If they think of even one more thing teachers are supposed to do, I'm sure we'll all just combust and go up in smoke."

He smiled at her grumbling humor and took it as encouragement, striding down the hall beside her.

"I have a few more things I have to see to here. Then I could come to your place. Or if you'd rather I could come later and take you to Toccoa or Clarkesville for dinner, maybe try Taylor's Trolley in Clarkesville. I bet you haven't eaten there."

"No. But I don't plan to go out tonight, Mr. Donovan. I'm going straight home and climb into my ugliest clothes and I don't intend to see anyone." She was shocked at how good it felt to be rude to him. Smiling her frostiest, she walked out, leaving him with a very surprised look on his face. If he thought he could treat her like a friend one day and last year's Easter egg the next, he'd better think again.

When really did climb into her ugliest clothes. Mrs. Haburn was busy making delightful gingerbread boys, but she didn't seem to need any help so Connie gratefully went to the pond alone, that is, with only the cat.

She sat down in Mrs. Haburn's rusty old chair out on the dock and watched the water for thirty minutes until its peaceful influence began to invade her being. Looking at trees rippled upside down, tiny waves from a winter wind or from stray leaves skidding onto the pond's surface, and the trace of a bubble path where a turtle swam helped her get things back into proper perspective. Whatever proper perspective was. She only knew that Maury Donovan was not a man she should lose her heart to, and she hoped she hadn't already done it.

The sun was going down. Long dark shadows enveloped the little valley. She was thinking how everything turned purple as night was coming on when a flash of light arrested her attention. Light shot into rainbow colors for a second off a windshield as a vehicle turned in at Mrs. Haburn's driveway. She thought someone was using the road to turn around, then realized it was Maury's blue pickup. Her heart thudded with instant hope before she scolded herself. Well, if he really wanted to see her, he could come all the way to the pond. She wasn't budging.

However, as he approached, she did get up and met him on shore. She felt too vulnerable sitting alone in that chair on the dock.

He held a hand up as if to defend himself. "I know you said not to come. But I had to."

"Well, I was just getting ready to walk. Come on. We'll circle the pond five times."

"That's my limit?"

"It'll be dark by then."

"I don't mind darkness. Stars will be out tonight." By now they'd made half the first round and he was actually having to speed up to keep in step with her.

"I met your mother yesterday," she said, taking control of the conversation.

He exhaled noisily. "You talked to her?"

"No. But she was talking about you. A very nice looking woman with short grayish hair. She looked a little like you, I think. She's proud of you, Maury."

"For no reason. And she's definitely not always proud. There's one whole part of me she wants nothing to do with."

"What's that?" She looked at him for the first time as they approached the dock and kept going around.

"My eternal desire to jump out of planes."

"Oh."

"She wants me to be stable, staid, and responsible. She wants me to be respected in the community. She wants me to be all that my father wasn't and much, much more. And she's afraid. Mainly she's afraid."

"Afraid?"

"Yes. She loved my father so very much and she lost him. She doesn't want to lose me, too."

"Did you tell her about Billy Ray? Do you talk to her about things that happen at school?"

"No. I do not!" His voice went harsh. They walked on in silence and the cat fell in behind them on their third round. By and by he said more softly, "I don't ever talk to my mother unless it's necessary, Connie. She and I just don't get along. She despises my flying and I must fly. That's why. . .that's why I'm afraid of you."

"Afraid of me?" She stopped. Blueberry bushes hunched down in purple rows behind him, and in the distance, the dark hill cut a stark shape out of a crimson sky. She couldn't see Maury's face very well, but she knew he was quite serious.

"I'm afraid because I can't give up flying, Connie. And any commitment I could make would require that. I don't think I can live without being able to fly and jump. It's my freedom, my joy."

"Who said you had to give it up to make a commitment? And who asked you to make any commitment?"

"Connie, you can tell how things are going. I. . .can't help myself when I'm around you. And the last thing in the world I want to do is hurt you."

"I see. Well, just walk on off then, Maury Donovan. Now. I don't understand why we're having this conversation. In case you think for some bizarre reason that I have some sort of feeling for you and you were about to hurt me, you can think again. I can take care of myself. And if you don't mind, *sir,* I'd like to finish this walk by myself. This warm dear cat is all I need." She scooped up the cat and marched on around the pond.

"Connie!" He grabbed her arm, she jerked it away. "Connie, I'm sorry if I said that all wrong. Look, I'm a big dunce."

"Yes, you are! For once you're absolutely right. You're a dunce because you think you can get away from commitments by hanging between earth and sky. Well, you can't!"

"Now wait a minute. I do make commitments. How do you think I keep a school running?"

"Not very well. That's how. You hate being a principal more than anything."

It was nearly dark now and in her fury she didn't notice the uneven spot along the bank. She tripped and would have probably tumbled down into the pond if Maury's strong arms hadn't caught her in an iron grip. She thought she heard bones cracking he squeezed her so hard. When he set her on a level surface and let her go, he stood still over her a minute, a towering dark figure, his face shadowed, his breathing uneven. Her last angry whiplash had taken the last spark out of her and now she wished she could take it all back. But it was too late. Maury Donovan grunted something that she didn't understand and walked briskly up the hill to his car where gravel spun under his tires as he left.

That know-it-all man! That infuriating, egotistical man! Why did I have the rotten luck to fall in love with someone I don't even like? She borrowed a hand from cuddling the cat to swipe at hot tears.

nine

The Christmas holidays were terribly long. Connie thought it would be so wonderful to be home learning about her sister's college experiences and sharing with Mother some of her problems with children. And, of course, visiting the neighbors, going to her own church, carrying fruit baskets to the shut-ins, and caroling on Christmas Eve. But this year nothing was the same. Her sister was furious with her for "doing Henry" so badly. Her parents didn't understand either, though her father did remind her, "To thine own self be true," implying that, understood or not, she had to stick to her own resolves.

And everywhere she went, whatever she was doing, Maury Donovan was never far from her thoughts, though she knew miserably that he wasn't thinking of her. If he had been, he would have done something about it by now, whether he was afraid of losing his freedom or not. After all those things she had said to him, he'd probably never give her one of those wonderful smiles again. She'd considered apologizing, but too much of what she'd said was true. She was only sorry she'd said it all, but she couldn't take it back. She'd have to do as he did and cover her feelings with activity.

Mother helped her create a touching bag, filled with cardboard letters and numbers and household objects to use in games with her slower children. She read thirstily from her new book by Gilbert Morris and from a volume of Robert Frost poetry, and she even helped give a birthday party for her eighty-year-old grandmother.

But still the days were far too long. She wondered what Mrs. Haburn was doing, and if her children from icy Maine had arrived home in time for Christmas. She was glad she'd finally confided in Mrs. Haburn her feelings for Maury Donovan. At least now someone knew, someone who would pray for her every day. She realized more than ever how important it was to have someone praying for her. Of course Mother would have prayed if she'd known. She was tempted to tell her, too, but it seemed as if one person knowing was all she could stand. How could she explain to Mother that she had fallen in love with the man about whom she'd written such irate letters?

She persuaded her parents she should go back to Mrs. Haburn's the Friday before school started. Her mother was really upset about it, but Connie's dad defended her, saying it would be a lot safer not to be traveling on Sunday at the end of a big holiday and, anyway, she needed time to get settled in before starting back to work.

Connie's reason for going back, if she were honest with herself, was a slight hope that she might catch a glimpse of Maury Donovan.

But the minute she turned into Mrs. Haburn's driveway, she knew she wasn't going to place herself anywhere that Maury Donovan might be until Sunday morning.

It started snowing after church Sunday. On the way home, flakes kissed the windshield, then whirled at them in fuzzy fury. Connie was thrilled, never having lived before where it snowed much. She was also glowing inside from the warmth of the big smile Maury had shot at her as he began the song service that morning. Maybe he would come over and walk in the snow with her.

Of course she knew he wouldn't. And he didn't. Not that day nor the next three days when the snow was so thick on the ground there was no getting up Mrs. Haburn's steep driveway. Good thing Mrs. Haburn had a healthy stack of wood on the porch for her kitchen heater. Even in that protected place, the women had to knock snow off the logs before bringing them in. The logs hissed with dampness when they were first added to the fire.

The kitchen table was a cozy spot for playing Scrabble, eating popcorn, and just talking over mugs of cocoa. Connie formed a snowman, complete with carrot nose and top hat. Mrs. Haburn, who wouldn't step past the porch, told all sorts of stories about the good old days when it was safe to eat snow cream and when the pond froze so thick a cow could cross it. All in all, it was a really wonderful time. But Connie was ecstatic when the sun came out.

The first few days back in school tried Connie's endurance considerably. All the children were like tightly wound tops, and by the end of the second week Connie was beginning to wonder if the rest of the year was going to be like that. All the excuses of too much candy, too much confinement, and too much spoiling had been worn out. When she woke in predawn darkness on Friday morning hearing rain on the roof, Connie groaned, buried her head deep in her pillow, then saw a vision of bright-cheeked children playing various homemade band instruments. She sat up in bed excited at the challenge. Yes! Today they would have a band. She'd been saving materials for just such an occasion.

Connie thought Maury Donovan would be tied up in a board meeting nearly all day, and besides, he hadn't stuck his head in her room once all week so why should he today? Anyway, the children needed some healthy outlet for their pent-up feelings, and she intended to make it available.

There were five drummers that day who made their drums from oatmeal boxes. Rob even held the drum she made for him and awkwardly beat on it. His ear-to-ear grin at hearing his own noise made Connie want to hug him. There was a little boy behind those blank eyes!

Marie was leader of the comb section because she could carry a tune so well. Combs encased in plastic wrap tickled children's lips as they hummed into them, making a sound not too dissimilar from the droning of bees.

Only five children made shakers with juice cans and dried pinto beans. But it sounded as if their whole wing of the building might just fall in. And all to the shuffle of six or seven sandblock creators.

The project was quite a success, even if Richard could never be persuaded to play a drum, shuffle sandblocks, or anything, and simply sat at his desk drawing spiders. Spiders were his thing to draw that day.

But success or not, an entire morning devoted to making and playing band instruments was not recognized as good teacher planning. When Mr. Donovan heard the ruckus coming from Miss Jensen's room, he steered his visiting board member toward the other end of the building. However, the noise was so obvious that the member, an elegant silver-haired woman, insisted they check in on it.

Connie would never forget the look on Maury Donovan's face when he opened her door that day. She saw his total surprise, followed by delight, quickly curtained by dismay and horror.

The children hadn't been happier all week. At that particular moment they were in excellent form, Connie thought, for they were marching in step to a lively recording of "The Grand Old Flag," with one little boy carrying the stars and stripes and everyone but Richard and Rob playing their new instruments. Desks were arranged so the band could wind among them, making a longer parade route, and Connie herself had gotten carried away at the moment and was standing up on one desk, directing. She used a fly swatter for a baton, that being the best she could lay her hands on quickly.

Connie left her directing to meet her guests, but she didn't stop the band from playing until Mr. Donovan yelled at her with the voice of an enraged bull. His thunder scared their visitor almost as much as it did Connie, but the children kept on marching. However, Connie was able to have them in their seats and quiet in less than sixty seconds and that so impressed the silver-haired woman she forgave her for her light approach to teaching. Of course Connie didn't hear the woman tell Mr. Donovan that he was to be commended for allowing teachers of various personalities some freedom. If she had, she would have understood even less why he was such a bear about the whole thing.

When Connie responded to Mr. Donovan's summons and sat before his desk, she saw no humor around his mouth nor in his sky blue eyes.

"I thought we understood each other about teaching methods, Miss Jensen."

"Yes, sir. But the children have been extremely restless all week and sometimes you just have to let them relax."

"They can relax when they get home to their cartoons," he said in a blistering voice. "Relaxing them is not our job. Our job is to be sure every one of them knows how to read!"

"Oh, but they do. All of them are doing pretty well now except Richard and, of course, Rob. Speaking of Richard reminds me. . . . What's this about Billy Ray being moved to another foster home? Are his parents making inquiries? When can he come back here?"

"Miss Jensen, do not try to swerve from the subject! Oh, dear, what was I talking about?" He wearily drew a hand across his forehead.

She smiled benignly and slid to the front of her seat. "I was asking about Billy Ray, Mr. Donovan. When do you think he could come back?"

Mr. Donovan swiveled his chair toward a window behind him and dropped his dark head into his hands. His shoulders vibrated like a pecan tree having its nuts shaken down. He was laughing at her! Well, that was better by far than anger. When he finally turned, he'd mustered some semblance of solemnity, but his eyes were moist.

"Billy Ray is better off where he is. His teacher is an acquaintance of mine, really a good man. And, no, I don't know when Billy Ray will get out. The disciplinary committee wouldn't allow me to negotiate with them at all. Lots of times children are in Alpine for a whole year, but usually at least half a year. Anyway, as I said, he's actually better off where he is."

"You don't really believe that. You don't believe Billy Ray is better off where he is. You've seen my children's scores and you know very well they're improving remarkably. Oh, sure, I make mistakes. That parade was out of line—actually, they were in step very well, if I do say so—and I won't digress like that again. But you can't believe Billy Ray is better off in a school where he's bound to be hearing curse words from other ill-reared children, where he must arrive every morning convinced he's a doomed and terrible child."

"Miss Jensen! Hey, that's not the way it is at Alpine. If you will just listen a minute! Calm down, will you?" He had come around the desk and propped on the edge of it, looking down at her with a worried frown. "Hey, don't go to pieces on me. I'm counting on you. Listen now. You want to visit Billy Ray? I'll give you the new directions, okay?"

When she left there several minutes later with directions in her hand, she felt giddy with relief. Not that she'd escaped Maury Donovan's lecture on impromptu bands, but because she was going again to see the little boy who'd so oddly won her affection. And because Maury cared enough to help her, even if it were only professional caring.

❧

She began visiting Billy Ray regularly, every Wednesday afternoon. He'd never trusted her, but she hoped that would change. At least he devoured Mrs. Haburn's huge tea cakes she took him. That first visit, Connie took a dozen cookies, thinking he could save some for his foster brothers and sisters. He ate all twelve in her presence. After he'd eaten six she began pleading with him to share, but he grunted that they were his and he wanted to eat them himself. She worried all the way home that he might have gotten sick. Next time she took only six. He looked very disappointed when he opened the box and ate the six as quickly as Connie might eat one. It was on the third visit he began to talk a little.

"I don't like this place."

"I know. I don't either."

"But you should like it," he said looking up at her with those wide blue eyes.

"Why should I like it?"

"Because you're a grownup. Grownups like all bad and awful stuff."

She smiled. "Sorry, Billy Ray. I guess I'm odd. I don't like this place because you're not happy here. Can you tell me why you're not happy here?"

He considered a minute as he played with a napkin his foster mother had laid by his frosted juice before she'd gone out with the other children. "Well. It's a nice place. No one whips me. Nothin' like that. Just that. . .I do miss my fam'ly. An' I don't like bein' so clean. We have to take a bath *every* night!"

Connie choked back a giggle. "I'll do my best to get you back to Pine Ridge. No promises about the baths, though. Are you being very exceptionally unbelievably good?"

He was scornful. "You know I'm not."

"Well, I want you to be. That's how you'll get to go home, see? And I want you back in my classroom. I miss you, Billy Ray. I need you to help me with Richard. He's been so—"

"Don't you say a bad word about my cousin!" The calm blue eyes blazed.

"Okay, okay. But I'm worried about Richard. I want to help him. And I know you could make the difference."

"How's. . .Mr. Donovan? I thought he'd come to see me. Last foster home they put me in, he came."

Something stirred in Connie's brain.

"Oh, you know principals," she said. "They have so much to worry about. But he remembers you. He made arrangements for me to come."

"I'd rather he'd come himself. Is he gone flying instead?"

"Flying! How do you know about that?" Connie closed the magazine she'd been flipping through.

"He has pictures on his walls. He flies and he jumps with parachutes. He's a really brave man."

&

In bed that night, Connie thought about what Billy Ray had said, that Mr. Donovan was a "really brave man." Maybe he was brave, but bravery in the skies wasn't doing Billy Ray any good while he stayed cooped up in that little house and cramped yard so far from his family and from his pet chicken. She must persuade Maury Donovan that he needed to visit the little boy again. It would do Billy Ray so much good to see his hero, to know he cared that much.

But apparently Mr. Donovan didn't care that much. Connie couldn't get any commitment out of him for a one-hour visit. She used the guilt complex angle, the pleading pose, the all-American-duty argument, but all to no avail.

But Billy Ray would still see his hero. She'd cooked up a scheme that would help her feelings as well as Billy Ray's, she hoped.

It had stung her over and over, thinking of Maury Donovan assuming that she might be falling for him. On top of that was the implication that of course she would "make him" stop sky diving if they were engaged. Such a male chauvinist, right here in the 1990s! He should have lived in the 1890s instead, except then his sky diving thrills might have been a bit tamer.

Would she be afraid for Maury to sky dive if she were engaged to him? Probably so. But she hoped she might be like Betty Friedman and have faith when the time came. Not that she thought that time was coming. Somehow, though, it was important to prove to Maury Donovan that flying was not such an all-powerful big deal to her. The only way to prove how she might react would be to place herself once again in the middle of action. Only this time, she'd get closer to the action. She'd fly with the pilot and take pictures of the jumpers as they left the plane. And she'd have lots of colorful pictures to give Billy Ray to have for his very own.

She was so pleased with her plan that she could hardly contain her excitement as she purchased fast film and a new zoom lens. For practice, she took a zillion pictures of the children swinging, running, and climbing on the playground. She visited photo shops, bugging owners with her questions, and even audited a class at North Georgia Tech in Clarkesville for several weeks. In the meantime, she tracked down Betty and Jock Friedman and talked them into letting her try her scheme. Of course she only told them she wanted pictures for Billy Ray. They could think whatever else they wanted to, but she did ask them not to tell anyone her plan, not even Maury Donovan. They were really nice folks and she believed they'd keep her secret.

❧

When the appointed Saturday in early March finally arrived, Connie's eyes only blinked once at dawning light before she bounced out of bed and ran to her front window to see if there was fog on her mountain. All she saw were baby clouds that would soon burn off. She dressed in a hurry, explained to Mrs. Haburn she had a busy day in Toccoa, and moved on without even any breakfast. She thought that not eating would be prudent.

Mrs. Haburn watched half-hidden behind a curtain, as Connie left. What could she be up to? If Connie weren't such a sweet Christian, Mrs. Haburn would almost think she were a criminal the way she'd been sneaking around. Connie had made sure Mrs. Haburn had her grocery list ready on Friday this week and they'd already been to town. So she couldn't complain. But no one could stop her from wondering and worrying. This sudden trip had to have something to do with that unpredictable Maury Donovan.

She'd warned Connie from the very start about Maury Donovan, but only as a principal, not dreaming she'd develop any deeper relationship. Granted, he was really quite appealing in a rough kind of way. There was something about him she just couldn't help liking herself. But he was mixed up. Didn't seem to have his life in focus.

"Guess I'm awful picky, Lord," Mrs. Haburn whispered. "Henry is stable and focused, even if on himself. And we didn't want him. But this man. He's gonna break Connie's heart. I feel it. But, dear Lord, as old as I am, you'd think I'd remember to ask for help and quit worryin'. I guess I'll never learn, hmmm?" She eased her aching knees to a rag rug before a well-worn old stuffed chair and continued talking out loud, the cat coming to purr ecstatically, curling around one sweatered elbow.

Connie turned on her radio to hear the weather news as she headed toward Gainesville. Seemed silly going so far to get on the plane. Since Maury and his friends would jump over Toccoa's airport this time, why didn't they get on the plane there? But Jock's plane was in Gainesville. He said they would all start together there.

"Clear, beautiful skies," chatted the weatherman, "perfect day for doing whatever makes you happy. Plant those bulbs. Cut your firewood. Enjoy the sunshine while you can." She smiled. Planting bulbs was what she should be doing. But instead, she was going flying!

She was scared and excited. Was this a tiny bit of how Maury might feel about now? Almost unconsciously she began to sing the old hymn Maury seemed to like so much: "There's a land that is fairer than day, and by faith I can see it afar, for the Father waits over the way, To prepare us a dwelling place there. In the sweet by and by. . ."

ten

Jock Friedman hadn't been happy about Connie's flying with him that day. But letting her go had seemed the human thing to do. And Jock was a warmhearted individual who didn't say no unless he absolutely had to. He should have told Maury about it, though. That was the least he could have done for his friend to save him from the jolt as they were all boarding. Maury either hated her dreadfully or loved her, Jock was sure, for his tan turned to chalk and he almost jerked the woman's arm off trying to get her out of the plane.

This was the teacher Maury had told him about, the one he'd groaned over as he told his friend, "What if this is the one? But I can't give everything up just now. I'm not ready." Jock grinned, remembering. Could be his friend, Maury, had finally been stung enough he'd realize some things are worth making arrangements for. Of course Jock couldn't say very much about that because his Betty had made all the adaptations in their life. But right now he'd leave the sky and never sweep it again if that's what it took to keep Betty.

As he looked down on apple orchards, pastures, and sprawling developments, he wondered why all the jumpers were so quiet. They couldn't communicate without shouting because of the wind noise caused by the large opening ready for them to exit. But they usually tried, or some did. He'd never flown such a quiet group as this. He glanced around and saw only stony faces. All of them were angry. Oh, boy. And the woman his wife had talked him into flying, Connie Jensen, was white as bleached sheets.

"Get her a baggy, will you, Maury?" he barked. It was the most humiliating moment in Connie's life. And there was more to come.

She blamed her sickness, not only on the throbbing motion, but also on the heat. It was so nauseatingly hot in that plane. She managed to get her jacket off, but the nausea clung to her until she felt weak as melted butter. Or maybe it was the noise. It was such a pounding shuddering noise made by wind beating around the large door opening. Or was the bright light making her sick? The searing intensity of it invaded her completely. She couldn't wear dark glasses and take pictures and so the light pinned her in place like a speared butterfly. Grabbing the baggy again, she lost the breakfast she hadn't eaten and thought limply that this was far worse than being seasick.

She heard Jock's shouts pointing out landmarks as they approached Toccoa—Lake Louise, Hartwell Lake Road, Tugalo Reservoir, Currahee Mountain—and she tried with rubbery fingers to get her camera ready. Sick or not, she'd get these pictures. She wouldn't let a little nausea stop her. She snapped a few pictures of the jumpers lining up. It was an awesome thing, sixteen men lining up in the seatless DC-3. Of course there wasn't room for one straight line so they wove their line, or lines. Every man knew exactly where he belonged.

One jumper knelt on the floor of the plane by the door on the left side of the fuselage near the tail. Periodically, he stuck his head out the opening into the wind stream and looked down at the ground. Jock had just told them they were flying at 10,500 feet. When this jumper kept sticking his head out, Connie was forced to use her baggy again. Seeing his face out in the wind stream was worse than a ghost movie; his skin actually blew so his cheeks looked hollow and folds appeared near his eyes and side-burns. Twice he signaled Jock to turn the plane slightly, then finally yelled, "Cut!"

As Jock pulled back the throttle on the engine, the spotter, as they called him, grasped the front inner edge of the door frame and swung his body outside the plane. Connie clung to her camera as if it could save her and tried closing her eyes tightly, but opened them again in spite of herself. What next?

In seconds there were three men outside the plane, clinging to edges of the opening with bare hands. This was worse than any nightmare Connie had ever had. She tried to remember why she'd had this harebrained idea and couldn't. But she took pictures. It was the only way to keep from fainting.

Teeth chattering from nervousness, Connie cautiously took a look at the faces of the men lined up inside the plane. They were all perfectly quiet, each one staring straight ahead, each suited in bold-colored nylon, some with a tight fitting sort of headgear with goggles, others bareheaded. Each jumper pressed his chest and arms tightly against the beach pack or parachute of the one in front of him and stood with his left foot forward and right foot behind. All this was as Jock had explained it to her with diagrams many hours ago on safe earth. She wanted Maury to look at her. Just once. But he was like a person in a trance, his eyes trained on the man ahead of him.

The very last jumper in line, a short, small man with a crewcut, suddenly snapped, "Hot!" Connie couldn't agree more, but realized immediately that was a code word. Now the jumpers were rocking and yelling, "Ready! Set! Go!" As they rocked, the middle floater, one of the three men outside the plane, pushed his hips farther out into the airstream, then rocked back toward the inside, pulling himself by the door frame, then out again. All the jumpers rocked simultaneously toward the door, then back.

Connie clenched her bottom lip in terror. She was too scared now to be sick. The whole plane was rocking horribly and she herself was only a couple feet from the door. As everyone shouted, "Go!" she put her camera to her face and began clicking. In seconds, when all sixteen men were gone, she sagged forward in exhaustion.

"You all right, Connie?"

"Sure, Jock. Fine."

"I'll try to get you in position for some shots of their formations if I can. Hold tight."

"Don't worry," Connie breathed.

"You know, to them these seconds are a long time. You have a feeling of eternity when you're out there free falling. Sometimes you're flying horizontally with the earth and time stands still, though you're still going a good 110 miles an hour."

Connie sucked in air. "They're going. . .that fast?"

"Oh, sometimes 200 when flying vertically. But they'll slow to a mere 10 or 15 miles an hour when their canopies are up. But there now, Connie, if you'll lean near the opening you can get some shots of their sixteen-man diamond. She's a beaut! Oh, wow!"

Connie was glad Jock was so enthusiastic that he didn't notice how timid she was about getting near the door. She did see the diamond made up of men in bright suits holding to each other a little like children making angels in the snow. It was spellbinding, as were the subsequent four-man diamonds that formed out of that one. Perfect timing and maneuvering it was.

"Amazing, isn't it?" shouted Jock, letting out an involuntary yodel. "Only God could make creatures that coordinated!"

"Yes. Only God," said Connie. She guessed that about now Maury Donovan had that look of pure joy on his windblown face.

Connie wished as Jock landed the plane that she'd stayed on the ground and watched the formations from below. It would have been much prettier and a lot less harrowing. Her bravery had turned out to be purely wimpy, and she shuddered at what Maury must think of her now. Well, she'd tried. At least she'd have some pictures for Billy Ray, albeit wobbly and blurred.

Connie knew she must still look shaken when Betty Friedman, who had driven up to be part of the ground excitement, offered her a ride back to Gainesville to get her car. "But first we'll all have lunch together here in Toccoa," said Betty. "The celebration after the jump is my favorite part." Her brown eyes shone with inner light.

While the men got out of their suits, Connie and the Friedmans watched airport activities. Feeling still a bit queasy, Connie headed for the restroom and literally ran into the tall, spare lady she'd identified months earlier as Maury's mother. Stepping aside in confusion, mumbling apologies, Connie then moved toward the door, but the woman touched her arm.

"Wait," she said. "Didn't you fly today with my son? I thought I saw you getting on Maury Donovan's plane."

"Yes. Yes, I. . .I took pictures," answered Connie, glad her camera was still around her neck.

"Oh. I see. I don't suppose you'd be able to give him a message for me? I'm Mrs. Donovan, Maury's mother."

"How do you do? I'm Connie Jensen, a teacher at Pine Ridge."

"Yes, of course, I should have known," said Mrs. Donovan, seeming to make a quick assessment of Connie's appearance. "Will you give my son a message, please?"

"Why. . .yes. But he'll be back soon, I think. He's just changing."

Mrs. Donovan nodded impatiently. "Tell him I'll expect him for supper tonight. About seven. I must run now."

"Sure. I'll tell him," said Connie, feeling stupid since Mrs. Donovan by then was several fast paces toward the outer door.

Inside the restroom, Connie stared at her pale, tousled look. No wonder Mrs. Donovan had eyed her so strangely. She pulled a brush from her bag and began to work at smoothing a million tangles out of her hair.

At Bell's Restaurant, Betty insisted on Connie's sitting at a table with her and Jock. They'd been seated only a moment when Maury slid into the fourth seat. His face was glowing with excitement as he turned to Connie exactly as if he'd never been grumpy or tried to throw her off the plane.

"How did you like it?" he asked.

"After I got through the ground attack it was really fine," said Connie, lifting her chin stubbornly.

"A bit airsick, weren't you?" Maury's mouth wasn't smiling, but his eyes were.

"Oh, she was quite plucky, that one," said Jock, setting his menu down. "I think she's already got her color back, don't you, Maury?"

"Don't tease the poor woman, you guys. She did do it, after all. That's more than can be said about me," said Betty wistfully, her full lips slightly pouting.

The next hour was so pleasant with Maury close by, exclaiming over the joys of free falling and successful formations, Connie almost forgot the message she was to deliver. When it came to her, she impulsively laid a hand on Maury's and leaned toward him.

"Did you know your mother was at the airport, Maury?"

"No. She couldn't have been. She doesn't ever come. It makes her very sick."

"But she was there. I met her."

His eyebrows went up. "You did?"

"Well. It was an accident. I ran into her." In spite of herself, Connie couldn't keep from giggling as she replayed the scene in her mind. "But anyway, she remembered seeing me get on your plane and she asked me to tell you to please come to supper about seven."

"You're sure she didn't say she'd *expect* me to come to supper?"

"Something like that," she agreed, folding her napkin.

Betty Friedman broke the silence that had fallen on them. "One of you guys get the waitress's attention. I want a big fattening dessert and some coffee. Connie, what would you like? Peach cobbler and ice cream? Or a hot fudge brownie?"

Connie groaned, then laughed. "Just coffee, I think."

Much later as Connie confessed the day's adventure to Mrs. Haburn, it occurred to her again how Mrs. Donovan's message had been like a splash of cold spring water on their party. Had she intended it that way? Or did she really want to rejoice with her son and just didn't know how? If she was afraid of flying, well, Connie could understand that part! But refusing to accept something as important as this was to Maury, that was another matter.

&

Soon after Connie retrieved her photos from the drugstore, she took them to Maury's office to show him. Though he'd teased her good-naturedly at the after-jump lunch, she didn't know for sure how her flight test had turned out until he looked at those pictures.

"I can't believe you really did that," he said, flipping through the stack of photos.

"Did what? Took such terrible pictures?"

"No. Went up with us that day. I. . .never realized it

would mean so much. Even if you did so generously feed the bag," he remembered with a chuckle.

She flushed self-consciously. "I was pretty disgusted with myself that day. For being such a wimp, you know."

"Connie you're so far from being a wimp, you wouldn't even know one if you saw one." He looked up from the pictures as he spoke and Connie saw admiration in his eyes. The horrors of the flight were well worth that look!

He glanced at a wall clock then and said, "Here, you better take these quick. I've got work to do here. Mrs. Gurdy is coming in a minute. But. . .oh, yes, by the way, when you deliver those to Billy Ray you'll need new directions." He put his hands behind his head and leaned back in his squeaky desk chair, looking smug.

"Why? Why new directions? *Another* foster home?"

"Yes. One near here. He's been so good, they're trans-ferring him back."

She squealed in excitement and clasped her hands to-gether. "Oh, thank you, thank you!" she exclaimed. "Tell me. Tell me right now where he is."

"You realize how much more work it will be for you having him here? And he's not the most grateful little guy I've seen!"

"Oh, but, Maury. . .Mr. Donovan. . .he wants to come back. He's going to be good because he wants to stay here. I really believe that boy's going to do something great someday."

"Well, I hope it's a good great. Hope he doesn't end up in the state pen. Anyway, I'll have to do as before and incorporate his studying into my office routine. Just pre-pare individual lesson plans for me to use, please, along the lines you're using with your other children right now, until we see how far he's progressed while he was gone."

"May I go see him today? It might help the transition."

"No. Because the fact remains Billy Ray did pull a knife on you. There's no kind of security at this foster home, and it's in a pretty remote area. I can't let you go, not yet."

She was going to ask him about the home, but Mrs. Gurdy came bustling in, her usual hat pushed back a little farther than usual. "Well, I guess you know your troublemaker's coming back," she announced, looking at Connie as she plopped into a winged chair.

"No. Just Billy Ray," murmured Connie and, with a parting look at Maury, she left.

As she hurried down the hall, questions zinged around in her head: What about Billy Ray's parents and the other children? Who had gotten Billy Ray freed from Alpine? Maury? What other secrets was he saving under that thick hair of his?

&

That week at church, several young adults were trying to organize a hike down into Tallulah Gorge before the weather got warm. They wanted Maury to be their guide. He'd done it before, they said, and knew the best way to go. Besides, according to several, Maury was the guy you'd want around if anything went wrong.

"And he's really a lot of fun, too," one young woman added, sounding a little defensive. Connie couldn't help smiling, thinking of Maury's moods of grim concentration that shadowed the moments when love of life itself shone from his face.

Maury agreed, with reservations. It meant pinning down a Saturday three weeks away, which might turn out to be a jewel of a flying Saturday, Connie knew. If a choice had to be made, she knew which way he'd go, and it wouldn't be hiking.

With growing excitement Connie looked forward to the hike. Maury had told her that afternoon months ago when they looked into the gorge that he'd show her the way down sometime. She'd like to have had him alone, but this was far better than nothing. After all, they'd both shied away from private meetings since his brutal pronouncement by the pond, thwarting something before it could begin. Connie still felt a strong pull between them, and she prayed every day that if Maury Donovan were the man for her, God would unkink the ropes that kept them knotted away from each other.

Billy Ray had turned into a model student. His foster mother sent him to school every day with his hair clean and combed and, after a few bouts with old classmates who'd forgotten how strong Billy Ray was, he began arriving with an unbloodied nose, too.

It was obvious to Connie that he nearly worshiped Maury Donovan. Billy Ray was even making progress in learning his addition facts with Mr. Donovan's strict rote teaching. He'd set Billy Ray to work, then be on the phone, working on his reams of paperwork, or even stepping down the hall to visit a classroom. Billy Ray would have the work done on time and brightly ask for more.

Sometimes Connie managed to leave her children with an aide long enough to play a game with Billy Ray using her touching bag of letters and numbers. But soon that was totally unnecessary. Billy Ray had broken the code.

Connie and Mrs. Haburn began picking Billy Ray up for Sunday school each week. Maury cautioned Connie not to get so involved with a pupil, then he himself began interesting Billy Ray in his boys' mission group. Billy Ray made quite an impression on teachers and children at church. For a while it looked as if they might have to leave him at home for the sake of other children who'd never heard such language at church. But he began improving, and Phil Stone insisted they give him more time.

"If the church can't minister to little guys like this, it's not much good, is it?" he asked.

Connie looked forward

"I guess I'll renew my contract," said Zena in the teachers' lounge one day. "At least I know sort of what's expected here."

"If we have the same principal next year," said Mrs. Gurdy.

Connie almost spilled her coffee. "What do you mean?" she blurted out.

"Why, I'm surprised you don't realize, as much as you've been in and out of Mr. Donovan's office. It's obvious a change is brewing. For one thing, his mother is on the board of education and if she got him this job, then I reckon she can move him to another as well. I know she's called him three times lately about something and she's not one of your chatty kind of people."

"I don't think that indicates he'd be making a change, Lora," put in one of the other teachers.

"No. But a visit from the superintendent with a prospective principal in tow might be."

"How could you know a man was a prospective principal?"

"I know one when I see one," said Mrs. Gurdy smugly. "And it wasn't a man, either."

Connie couldn't forget this conversation, though she'd never set great store on what Mrs. Gurdy said. Still, the woman did have an uncanny art for knowing things no one else had heard or seen. She'd probably have been a good police detective. Now Connie couldn't decide whether to sign her contract for another year. She'd never intended to stay more than one year, but where would Maury be and was there any hope he'd ever love her the way she loved him? If she left, there wouldn't be a chance. Yet if she stayed, she might just be asking for another year of misery.

She was thinking about this as she walked down the hall one afternoon responding to a call from the principal to come to his office. He hadn't raked her over the coals lately, and it was about time, she guessed. She'd taught Marie how to sew on buttons last week and probably he found out about that. Or he was upset because Richard, as bright as he seemed to be, still could not read other than the words *it, and, see,* and *I, me, you.*

When she walked into the office, she knew something was terribly wrong. And it wasn't just because Maury Donovan was standing at his window, staring out at the mountains. There was a heavy feeling in the air. She sat down quietly and waited a few minutes, then cleared her throat. He spun as if he'd been shot. His face had lines as deep as the gorge, lines that had not been there the day before, and his hair seemed extra black against his pale face. He touched the corner of his desk as he moved toward her, never releasing her from his gaze.

Pulling her to her feet, he held her against him and she felt him shaking. "It's Jock," he whispered hoarsely. "He crashed. In the mountains."

"Jock? But that can't be! He is so careful!"

"Careful isn't enough. Here, you better sit down."

"How? How did it happen?" Connie asked, dreading the details.

"I don't know except that he crashed in the mountains and he was dead when rescuers reached him. They called me because I was his best friend. They want me to. . . ."

"You have to tell Betty?"

He nodded and her own eyes stung with tears for both of them, for all of them. Dear Jock! So compassionate, funny, and bright! Gone. Just like that.

"Connie. . .please, . . .go with me."

"Yes. Of course I will."

It was the hardest thing she'd ever done in her life. But Betty made it easier for both of them. It was as if she'd always known it would happen sometime. She cried. But she didn't go into hysterics. In the end, she was down on her knees in front of Maury, comforting him, or trying to.

Maury couldn't be comforted. Betty wanted him to sing at the funeral, but he refused. Connie understood. It would have been entirely too hard. But she didn't understand the way Maury shut others out and withdrew into himself. He was a Christian, and Jock had been a Christian. Jock had died doing what he wanted to do. So what was there to be bitter about? And who was he bitter toward?

It sounded as if he thought God should have reached down and become pilot of the plane when Jock had his heart attack. Instead He had smiled from the sky and watched him fall. Maybe Maury felt that way about his father's death, too, as if God should have opened that bottle of medicine for him.

More and more distance formed between Maury Donovan and those around him. He was like a bear routed early out of hibernation or a cornered rattlesnake. The sunshine had left his eyes.

eleven

When Billy Ray was placed again in Connie's room, she was nervous. It wasn't that she was afraid of Billy Ray. She'd never believed Billy Ray felt personally malicious toward her anyway. She was nervous because she didn't want him to lose all the emotional ground he'd gained, and she wasn't sure how she should deal with him.

As far as that went, who did she know how to deal with? Quiet, bright Richard, who could make a beautiful picture of a kite, but couldn't spell it? Or Rob, who could only write his name on good days? Or Marie, who could read circles around everyone now and needed so much more challenge than time seemed to allow? Just as her mother had predicted, Connie felt that after a year's teaching she'd know less than she had when she started.

Connie had been shocked to learn from Maury that Billy Ray's whole family had moved and left no forwarding address. They hadn't taken his pet chicken. Worse than that. They'd left it to starve, and Maury had found it in the corner of its pen, a rotten mass of feathers. He'd had to report this to Billy Ray since he asked continually about his chicken. But the boy so adored Mr. Donovan that he had appeared to work through all this trauma and be happier than he'd ever been before.

Now, for whatever reason, Mr. Donovan canceled his sessions with Billy Ray. Mrs. Gurdy said she'd known all along he wouldn't stick to such a routine. What principal would, or should, as a matter of fact? A principal should do his job, teachers theirs. Connie personally was convinced it was because of Jock's death. He needed more time, she supposed. She wasn't Billy Ray's choice, but she'd have to do her best, that was all, whether Billy Ray liked it or not.

Most teachers had trouble with their pupils talking too much. That hadn't been Connie's trouble with Billy Ray before his suspension. It was when he hadn't talked he'd become frightening. Now, though, he seemed actually pretty glad to be back in his own desk at last. And he talked a lot.

He found he could get the attention of the whole class by telling stories he made up. Everyone's favorite was the tale about Billy Ray and his pa, killing a wildcat with their bare hands. Connie saw this storytelling as a building time and let him have a good bit of freedom. But she began to notice that more and more of his fantastic tales were centered around sky divers in some way or another.

"I know a sky diver myself," he concluded a story one day. "I'm not telling who it is, but I can tell you this. He's gonna let me go with him one of these days. Sometime I'll see him come whizzing down like Superman. Whoosh!" Billy Ray stood on his desk and demonstrated a quick descent to the delight of the other children.

"Okay, okay, Billy Ray," said Connie. "Enough of that now. Let's get back to when we use capital or upper case letters. If Billy Ray had been writing his story. . . ."

Another time Billy Ray confided in Connie as he stood

at her desk while she checked his workbook. "Mr. Donovan's gonna take me sky diving. He promised. You'll see, Miss Jensen."

"Sure, Billy Ray," she countered, trying to make light of it.

Had Maury really promised to take Billy Ray to watch the sky diving? She was sure he hadn't. Or hadn't meant to anyway. She needed to ask him, but nowadays there never seemed the right moment to ask him anything.

When she learned from Jean that Phil Stone had persuaded Maury to keep his promise to guide their young adult church group on a hike down into Tallulah Gorge, Connie was surprised and excited. He hadn't given up everything, after all. And surely that day she'd have a chance to ask him just what he'd promised Billy Ray.

❧

The day they'd chosen dawned chill, but clear and ice free. Mrs. Haburn grumbled good-naturedly as she prepared oatmeal and cheese toast. "Foolhardiest thing you've done yet, outside of flying in a plane with the door off. What will it be next? Planning any underwater adventures? Just don't tell me about 'em. You know, you're likely gonna break a leg and have to hobble around like me. Or break your head on a rock an' have to be spoon-fed rest o' yer life. Do you really want that?"

"No, ma'am." Connie laughed. She was in bubbling good spirits. "I'll be totally and absolutely careful. I promise."

As a person looking down from above becomes familiar with Tallulah Gorge's facial features, its rugged lines, idiosyncratic curves, its quirky smiles and frowns caused by differing light effects, the gorge becomes a very good acquaintance, a memorable character. But if a brave soul descends *into* the gorge, its very heart is exposed. This person learns not just what the gorge is like, but what it's made of, what makes it endure. And the acquaintance of surface comments becomes the friend of shared hopes.

This was the philosophy with which Maury entertained his group as he approached the gorge. Parking on a lonely promontory, he said jovially, "Here we are." He seemed more himself than he had in weeks.

They looked around dubiously. The road by which they'd neared the edge wasn't highly traveled. On this chilly morning no one else was around, only a lone hawk, circling against a blue sky. Before them a sign warned that those who descended the gorge did so at their own risk. "Maybe this isn't such a good idea," said one or two, peering over the precipice.

"Oh, come on, folks, you knew when we started out this wasn't the thing the general public does. We've got on the right shoes, Maury knows the way, let's go." Jean wasn't about to be stopped from this adventure.

The path Maury chose for them, the one most frequently used, he said, zigzagged down approximately two thousand feet to a rock-lined riverbed. Connie wasn't at all sure it could be called a path in the usual sense. It certainly wasn't a walking path, only a sliding one for stretching, sideways steps only! Bushes and wind-toughened trees, slickened by hundreds of hand grips, grew between scarred ancient rocks. A foothold here, a handhold there, were sometimes plain to see, sometimes hard to be imagined.

Connie was glad she'd chosen jeans rather than corduroy shorts. Her knees would have been raw by the time she got down if she hadn't. She paused and propped against a jutting rock to swipe her sweat shirt off, exposing her bright blue tee-shirt. Tying sweat shirt sleeves around her waist, she inched down to the next foothold.

"It's about as rugged a path as we can manage without needing special climbing equipment," Dave Olds remarked as he accidentally knocked dry leaves onto Connie's head.

"And I dread to think of pulling myself back up," said Connie, shaking trash out of her hair. "I'll be wishing I weighed about fifty pounds less. Is there any other way back up?"

"Don't think so," laughed Dave.

"Down by the power plant there's a rusty cable car," called Maury from below, "but we're coming back out on our own speed."

"Did you hear that, Dave?" Connie passed the message up.

"Tell him to speak for himself," said Dave.

Winded, hot, bruised, and scraped, the ten adults scrambled down over the last laurel-caressed black boulder, onto the canyon floor. Several sat down as soon as they could. Connie's knees were quivery, but she wobbled over to the water's edge to peer into a frothy pool fed by one of many small cascades. Staring at angry water made her dizzy, and she turned away only to find herself staring up at Maury's dark face. He smiled and put an arm around her to steady her.

"May not be that much water compared to what there was before 1910 or whenever they dammed the river, but it's more than you'd want to get trapped in." Maury glanced around at others who had ambled over, including them in his remarks.

"Trapped in?" asked Connie, glancing behind her.

"Yes. You get in one of these big holes and you can't get out, the sides are so steep and slick."

"Has that ever happened to anyone?" asked Jean, a touch of challenge in her voice.

"Yes, afraid so. A honeymoon couple a few years ago got in a pool. . .I suppose they thought it would be a nice whirlpool. Anyway, they never got out. They were found dead from exposure."

"Maury! You're making that up. No one found them for that long?" Dave wanted to know.

"There aren't that many people coming here all the time, so they had it to themselves for far too long. And you'd be surprised how quickly total exposure to harsh elements can deteriorate a person. All right, Dave, maybe I've got my story wrong a bit. Maybe there was a storm that made it worse. Anybody else remember?"

"Not exactly. But I remember it happening," spoke up one of the others. "Seems things like that are always happening to honeymooners, doesn't it? Love is dangerous."

"Can be," said Jean, cutting her eyes toward Connie and Maury.

"On the other hand, love can rescue the perishing," quipped Dave with a grin at his own wit.

"And the main thing is, the gorge awaits us," said

Maury, waving a go-ahead signal as he strode off.

Maury's being abrupt was nothing new. Still Connie wondered if the teasing had goaded him into rushing on. She wanted to hide her own pink blush and only hoped that anyone who might have noticed would blame it on exertion.

While the trail into the gorge hadn't been a walking trail, the one downstream was nonexistent. Since there was nothing but rock and water, there was little to call a path. Maury's long legs stretched easily from one rock to another over rushing water and the rest followed, not daring to lag behind for fear they'd get stranded. It reminded Connie of following a maze. Some ways seemed as good as others, but the wrong choice could lead you to a dead end. She had to do some fast thinking, as well as use fast footwork, to keep up.

She kept wishing there was time to stop and feel the unbelievable, perfectly round, smooth craters in some of the rocks that had been shaped, Maury told them, by pebbles and water beating rhythms on them for hundreds of years. But there was no time to pause until they finally came to a wide, solid rock beach that slanted toward the base of the cliff.

"There's the old lookout building, way up above us," said Jean, head tilted back. "I remember coming there when I was little. That was the main road then. Mama used to give my brother and me each a dime to look through the telescope."

"Yeah. Me, too," said one of the other women. "I can't believe I'm looking up at it from so far below. My mother wouldn't have dared let me do this. Still wouldn't if she knew," she giggled. "Oh, look, is that a weasel, Maury? I know that's a weasel!"

Maury and others watched with bated breath as the long furry creature slid out from a stunted laurel on the other side of the water, looked around, then slunk back into hiding.

"That's a weasel, all right," pronounced Maury, and Connie wondered to herself if there was anything he didn't know.

Connie found another perfect rock hole the size of a basketball and sat down beside it to run her hand around in its smoothness. Funny how the mere feel of something could be soothing, calming. Wouldn't she love it if her school children could have in their playground just one enormous wonderful rock like this with mysterious craters! But even if such a rock were available, there'd be some safety regulation against it.

"I've always wanted to come down here," said Jean, sitting down beside Connie. "Maury's right. There have been some pretty grim stories of awful things happening to people who didn't use good judgment. But isn't it beautiful down here!" She lay back on the hard floor, the better to enjoy watching the sky framed by pine-trimmed edges of canyon far above.

"It is beautiful. It's wonderful!" agreed Connie.

"Connie! Jean! Come on, let's go on down farther. Maury says watch out for ghosts. Aren't you coming?"

The women looked at each other and laughed. "We're afraid of ghosts!" Jean answered. "Besides," she added to Connie, "I'd just like to slow down and absorb some of this."

"I know." Connie lay back beside her friend, shielding her eyes with one arm, idly watching birds circling halfway up the depth of the gorge. To which world did those birds belong? Were they below their world or above it? Probably they could live in either or both. Did Maury know some of their freedom when he floated earthward at a dreamy ten miles per hour?

When another member of the group pulled Jean to her feet, insisting she go with them, Connie stayed where she was. Adventure was exciting, but she could do with some absorbing as Jean called it. A gust of wind blew down the canyon and Connie shivered as she pulled her sweat shirt back on. It didn't take long when you stopped moving to realize the air wasn't so warm after all. Stretching out on the natural pavement, she drew a sigh of contentment.

"Can you imagine it in a month or two with all those laurels and rhododendrons blooming?" asked Maury, startling her so she almost jerked a knot in her neck.

"It must be glorious," she said, recovering her composure, at least outwardly. "More than glorious because it already is that. Didn't the others need you to guide them down the gorge? What was that about ghosts?"

"Oh, Dave has my instructions. They don't need me. As to the ghosts. . .you may never know." His grin was full of mischief.

"And I suppose you think you've raised my curiosity now and I'm going to go leaping down the canyon."

"I hope not," he said. "Sitting here on the beach beside you is vastly more appealing than running after you right now."

She covered her crimson face with both hands, then peered between her fingers at the bulk of him sitting so very near, apparently engrossed in studying the sky.

"Since you're our guide, tell me what it was like here, back at the turn of the century."

"Well, terribly busy. Hotels, several of them, full in season. A train affectionately called the TF, making a run every day. Big spenders coming from all over the world. It was the place to be. And Wallenda in the '70s wasn't the first to walk across it on tightrope, you know. There was a tightrope walker back in 1915 or something who was paid by a big hotel to come walk across. My grandmother remembered that."

"Your grandmother?"

"Yes. She died five years ago. And, speaking of bustling, I can remember myself, as Jean does, when that lookout building up there was as busy as a shopping center."

"Wow! And you look so young," she teased him as she sat up. She pushed her hair behind her ears, then flipped the glistening length of it over her shoulders, all the time watching his smile involve every groove and plane on his face.

"You idiot," he said, a warm light in his eyes.

Neither of them spoke for a few minutes, just enjoying sounds of rushing water, a leaf sliding across rock, the faraway drone of a plane. And each other. Then perhaps the plane reminded Maury of Jock. A shadow fell across his face.

"This place always makes me think of the song 'Rock of Ages.' I need to be able to hide myself in that Rock about now."

"Can't you?"

He ignored her question. "You know, it could be my time to go next."

The air was charged with question marks. What did he expect her to say?

She took a deep breath. "Sure. It might be me, too. Knifed by one of my students."

"But you'd be doing your job."

"Yes. I'd be doing my job."

"I'd be out having fun if I died sky diving. My mother says it's an unreasonable risk."

"Well. I guess she's kind of right, isn't she? Depends on what angle you look from. Your mother's called you then?"

"Oh, yes. Several times lately."

"Do you think you should stop sky diving, Maury?"

"No! I'm not stopping!" She was shaken by the harshness in his voice. "I'd be only a shadow of myself without sky diving. That's where I get my inspiration. That's where I'm really me."

"Maybe you're looking at the wrong place for your inspiration," said Connie, leaning over her knees so her hair fell around her like a curtain.

"Maybe. I've been thinking the same thing. Maybe I've been worshiping creations instead of the Creator. But, Connie, I'm so confused right now I can't sort it all out."

"You will. I know you will."

"I'm glad you know it." He stood and shoved hands deeply into his pockets.

"Remember, God gives songs even in the night, Maury. I read that in Psalms not long ago. This is a night for you, but maybe you'll find a beautiful song in it."

"You should be a poet, the way you think," he said, turning gentle again as he knelt and reached for her hand. "Connie, I have to make a change. I can't go on fighting within myself all the time, feeling like a hypocrite half the time, a misfit the rest of the time. I know you're not going to understand this."

Her mind raced ahead of him. So he was giving up the principal's job. Mrs. Gurdy was right. Well, wasn't this what she'd prayed for? That he'd be put in the right spot? But now she didn't want him to leave.

"Connie, did you hear me?"

"I'm sorry, Maury, what?"

"I said I'm giving up my church job."

"Your church job? The one you love most?"

"Who said I loved it most?"

"I did." She stood up. "Maury, you can't!"

"I can. I already talked to Phil Stone."

"Maury, why?" The intensity of her question was written all over her face. To her it seemed as if her question echoed back and forth, clanging against walls of the canyon.

"I've got to become focused," answered Maury. "I've done a terrible job this year, as you well know. There are children in every grade who can hardly read road signs, much less anything else. I've got to do better."

"Quitting your music job is going to make that right?"

"I need more time to take special courses, make more resources available to teachers. You know what a rat race it is, Connie. Besides, you know I couldn't make it on my part-time musician's salary. I can't give up my school job."

"This isn't about money, and you know it."

"What then?" His eyebrows shot up.

"It's about a debt, but not a monetary one."

His jaw was firm, his arms across his chest. "I suppose you're beginning to use your psychology on me now. Well, would you explain what you're talking about?"

She took a deep breath. "Maury Donovan, if you could teach every child in Georgia how to read, it wouldn't bring your father back. Don't you know that?"

His eyes widened as if she'd struck him. "That's not what I'm doing. That's got nothing to do with it."

"Yes, it does, it most certainly does. And maybe teaching every child to read is a worthy goal, but your motive is not. Your heart isn't in teaching or administering, certainly not administering. And I don't think God asked you to do something you don't have a heart for."

"Oh, you don't, do you?" He gripped both her arms and stared deep into her eyes. "Just what business did you have coming along, confusing me so, anyway? I knew where I was going and everything until you walked into my office."

"Well," she held his gaze steadfastly, then whispered, "maybe I'll be gone soon."

He sighed. "I knew you wouldn't like my decision. I don't like all of it myself, mainly because. . . . I know you've realized how I feel about you. You'd have to. And I wish more than anything—"

"What, Maury? What do you wish more than any-hing?" Her face had gone from a flushed pink to white.

"That I could answer that question," he answered. "If only I knew the one thing I wanted more than anything."

She looked down at the toes of her hiking shoes and dabbed at a tear behind the drift of her hair. "You will someday," she said firmly. "I think I should be honored you cared enough to tell me a second time that you don't want to care. Somehow right now it doesn't feel particularly good."

"Connie." His hands were warm on her shoulders and she looked up because she couldn't help herself. She'd never before realized his eyes held varying shades of bluish lakes, each with many depths. "Whatever you think about me, know this. I want the very best for you. Contrary to the way I came across in September, I think you're a jam-up person, yes, a jam-up teacher, and I'd recommend you to anyone."

"Of course you'd send along a bottle of aspirin for my next boss, too, I suppose," she said with a grin as she heard their noisy friends returning up the canyon.

"The biggest bottle I could find," he said, letting his hands slide down her arms before he turned away.

"Maury, you clown, nary a ghost lured us into that rusty cable car!" Dave yelled before they could even see him.

"Yeah, Maury, you promised us ghosts!" cried Jean.

"Didn't you see the wreck hanging from a tree above you? Now wouldn't you think there'd be a ghost floating around somewhere? Tell me how anybody got out of that car alive or dead? And I see you found yourself a sign."

" 'Men At Work.' Don't you just love it?" yodeled Dave, lugging an orange caution sign rusted by years and weather. "I'm going to put this up outside my garage."

"Oh, boy, what a lie that will be," muttered Jean, and everyone laughed.

Maury pointed out to them the exact spots where Wallenda's cable had been attached, while they munched on candy bars he magically pulled out of a small pack. For Connie, the sweet candy might just as well have been bitter medicine. She was glad when they began the strenuous climb out.

As she stretched herself beyond what she thought she could and dragged herself up over impossible spots, her mind kept returning to things Maury had said, such as "I knew you wouldn't approve of this," meaning his giving up the church job. How had he known that about her? But it was so true. "Oh, Maury, no, please, you're dropping the wrong job!" she wanted to plead. But her main plea was, "Maury, don't shut me out!"

Back home, sitting on her log in the woods above the pond, she realized soberly what she'd learned about herself. She wanted to marry a man who put God first. Henry didn't put God first. Neither did Maury.

"But I love Maury," she whispered in the shadows.

It was Monday morning before it dawned on her she'd never asked Maury if he'd promised to take Billy Ray to watch sky diving.

twelve

The month of May progressed rapidly. Connie felt like a piece of birch bark in a time river approaching a mighty waterfall, with nothing to stop her from plunging over in the powerful rush of water. On the other hand, time froze in cameo segments. She would always be grading papers at her book-crammed desk at Mrs. Haburn's, looking up now and again to see the picture of prayers in a field. Or she would always be listening to Joyce and Marie, Sammy, and others, reading their very first "chapter" books. She would always, all her life, be settling Rob in his chair one more time.

Blueberry bushes bloomed. Connie hadn't ever considered how blueberry flowers might look. They were tiny, pinkish bells, very dainty, but the most amazing thing was their profusion. If all those flowers developed into berries. . . . Well, it was no wonder Mrs. Haburn could sell so many, make pies, and still can, jam, and freeze quarts and quarts of berries.

Outside Connie's bedroom window, "her" maple tree threw leaf shadows again like delicate hands against her curtain. On the hillside beyond the road, glossy laurel bushes were decorated with puffy clusters of faint pink umbels and rhododendrons bloomed. Wild azalea, or honeysuckle, as Mrs. Haburn called it, flamed orange and lemon in the woods.

Connie hadn't signed her contract for the next year. She knew she couldn't teach under Maury Donovan another year. Instead, she accepted a position in Augusta and was back and forth several weekends, making arrangements. It was going to be nice to be near home again, she told herself. One weekend when she and her mother were talking, she spilled out her feelings about Maury Donovan.

"I was wrong to try to persuade you to marry Henry when you didn't love him," said Mrs. Jensen. "And now you've learned what the other side of unreturned love is like. I'm truly sorry."

"It isn't even that simple," said Connie. "If it were unreturned love, I could accept it more easily, I think. But he loves me, Mother, he does love me! Yet he will not commit himself because. . . ."

"Because?"

"Because he thinks he'd have to give up his dangerous adventuring if he married. And I think, more than that maybe, I don't know, he's decided on a course of life and he doesn't want me or the Lord changing it for him."

"I wish we could have met him. I'm sure he's a really good man. You said he has this thing, this mighty cause, to be sure the children learn to read. And that is a wonderful cause, Connie!"

"Sure. But he's let the cause become more important than the children. And he works so hard with so little joy. It just doesn't seem as if he were meant for that job."

"But he has to decide that."

"And he has. He's decided about the job and about me."

"Oh, dear! I am sorry. But I'm glad you're coming back here."

"Me, too. But I'll miss Mrs. Haburn so much."

Mrs. Jensen's eyes darkened. "She's been a better mother than I have been."

"No, Mother, don't say that! She was simply herself, a really wonderful woman, always there when I needed her. And I don't know why I'm talking in the past tense. I have two more weeks of school."

Two more weeks! Only two more weeks to teach "her" children. It would be a relief in some ways. But. . .

"I wish I knew what to do for Billy Ray, Mom. He was a different child for a while when I was taking him to church and Maury was working with him. At first when I took him to Sunday morning church, I had to keep close watch to keep him from making spitballs out of my bulletin. Then, later on, he really began to listen, I thought. But now since Maury resigned all his jobs at church and doesn't even go anymore, neither does Billy Ray want to go. Worse than that, he's up to his old tricks at school. Friday he stole Marie's homework and tore it to shreds right in front of us all—just pure meanness."

"From all you've told me, you're doing everything there is to do, Connie. You have helped him an awful lot. Remember that."

"Yes. But it's not good enough. I don't want to leave him unhappy. I tried to get him to play his harmonica the other day and, after several refusals, he finally said he'd buried it."

"Buried it?"

"Yes. Said he would never play it again and when I said he just had to, he said Mr. Donovan doesn't sing anymore so he doesn't play harmonica anymore. What could I say?"

"Honey, be careful. I'm really not sure that boy should still be free after his attack on you."

"Oh, Mother, I'm not afraid of him! I'm just afraid for him."

❧

It was the last week of school and the children were incredibly loud and unmanageable. One day in the midst of reading exercises that weren't exciting even the brighter students, Connie suddenly clapped her hands for attention and announced they should put their books and papers all away. Startled little faces stared back at her.

"I mean it. Put them away," she said. "We're going to make something instead. Puppets." She went to the storage room and came back with a stack of paper plates and a package of tongue depressors. "I want you each to make a puppet of who you'd like to be. Think real hard first of who you'd really, really like to be. You can make a puppet of a famous person you admire, or you can make one of, let me see, a fireman, a policeman, the president, a secretary—"

"A teacher?" asked Marie.

"Sure."

"A car thief?" asked Billy Ray without a smile.

She gave him an evil look and ignored his question. "When you've finished your puppet, class, I want you to be ready to put it up in front of your face and tell us about yourself, the puppet self, the one you would like most to be. Okay? Now get your crayons out and do your very best job."

The children were as noisy as ever, but now they were at least accomplishing something. Connie sat down at her desk to work in her grade book, pleased that even Rob was occupied for the moment as he held a purple crayon awkwardly like an ice pick and slashed at the plate.

Feeling herself being closely watched, she raised her eyes to look into the solemn face of Billy Ray. After all these months, he could still slip up on her like a scout in moccasins. She narrowed her eyes. "What is it, Billy Ray? Why aren't you working on your puppet?"

"Don't need a stupid puppet. You know what I want to be."

He was holding his hand behind him. Now he was pulling it out. For one frozen second she pictured herself again with that knife coming at her. Then she realized what he held was a tightly folded piece of paper.

"What is that?" she asked, moistening her lips.

"It's a copy of Mr. Donovan's letter about the sky diving Saturday. I want you to take me. Please?"

"Where did you get that?"

"From Mr. Donovan's office. While he was gone I just made a copy, that's all. Please, Miss Jensen?"

"Billy Ray, you should *never* take things like that. It's stealing as sure as. . .stealing a car. And you've already asked me about going to see the sky diving." How many times had Billy Ray asked already? If only he knew how much she wished she could take him, but it was impossible. She wanted to get through this job and leave with as little contact with Mr. Donovan as possible.

"Why can't you?"

"Because. It's in Gainesville, a long ways. And I have so much to do, getting ready to move soon. Come on now. Why don't you make a puppet of a sky diver, Billy Ray. Maybe someday you can be one. You could join the air force like Mr. Donovan and. . . ."

Connie told Zena about the episode later on as they watched their children at play.

"If Billy Ray wants to see Mr. Donovan jump so badly, why don't you take him? You've done everything else for the boy. Or is it that you like Mr. Donovan too much to be in his vicinity?"

"Oh, Zena, I wish I could have taken your advice and never thought two things about that man!"

"Well," said Zena, rolling a candy wrapper into a tighter and tighter ball, "sometimes advice, particularly mine, is just totally lost on people. Anyway, this is a case of filling the big desire of one very underprivileged boy. If he'd asked me, he could just forget it because I don't do stuff like that. . .help people out, I mean. But you. . .You really will be sorry you didn't."

"Maybe so. I'll think about it. And, Zena. . .that's not true about you. You have helped me all year. I couldn't have made it without you."

Zena smiled brightly and began to call her children in. "Good luck!" she said over her shoulder.

⋙

Connie slept fitfully that night and woke early the next

morning. She sat by her window looking up through maple leaves to the dark tree line beyond the highway and the gray sky brightening the hillside's rim. A whippoorwill was singing down beyond the pond somewhere.

"Should I take him?" she whispered against the grayness at her window. "Maury would never believe I was just bringing Billy Ray. He'd think. . . . But what does it matter what he thinks? After next week I'll never see him again anyway. So I can have puppet shows and I can take Billy Ray to see the sky diving."

When Connie finally realized about nine o'clock that Billy Ray wasn't coming to school that day, she was relieved. Perhaps he had conveniently gotten sick for these last few days and she would be safe from his brooding, belligerent hurting and from taking him to Gainesville.

Maury Donovan came in while the children were waxing dramatic with their puppets. He stood rigidly near the door, a dark expression on his face. Connie moved toward him but paused to reseat Rob. When she stood again, Maury was gone. Her own disappointment rattled her. Even his lectures were better than nothing at all, she thought.

That afternoon Connie sat on the dock swinging her legs above slightly murky water while Mrs. Haburn fished. Occasionally she threw out crumbs for the ducks, who swam majestically about, their dark green and black feathers glistening in the sun.

"Had a letter from my daughter today. She's found another job."

"Oh. That's nice. I guess."

"Means she won't be coming here for the summer."

"And you'll have an empty house. Mrs. Haburn, I'm sorry—"

"Now, now, don't go being sorry for me. Lord's taken care of me every turn in my life. And He will this time, too. Still wish you could be here for blueberry season, though. You've never seen any prettier blueberries than mine. You can see the trees are plumb loaded down."

"Yes, and they'll be ripe before too long, won't they? Maybe—"

She didn't finish her sentence, for at that moment Maury Donovan's blue pickup flashed down the hill.

"Hmmm, wonder what he wants?" murmured Mrs. Haburn.

Connie jumped up and ran toward him, knowing instinctively that something must be badly wrong.

"You don't know anything about Billy Ray?" asked Maury.

"Billy Ray? No! I supposed he was sick. Why?"

"His foster mother says she sent him to school. He hasn't been home all day."

"Maybe he's gone hunting for his family."

"Maybe. Just wondered if you had any other clues. It's too early for the police to be very involved, you know, but I'm worried."

Connie wondered silently why he was worried now when he'd ignored Billy Ray for the last few weeks.

"Can you think of anything he's said that might help me find him?" urged Maury.

"Well, I know what he wanted to do more than anything. He's been asking me to take him and I kept telling him I couldn't. He wanted to see you sky dive Saturday. It's all he thought about."

"Oh. Do you think he might hitchhike? Would he know where to go?"

"He's awfully smart. Yes, I think he'd figure that out. He wouldn't realize how hard it would be to get thirty or forty miles. But he wanted to go so much, I don't think much of anything would stop him if he got started. I. . . had decided to take him, but he wasn't there today for me to tell him. I thought he must be sick."

"You know Billy Ray never gets sick," said Maury with no sympathy as he ran back to his truck.

"Maury, wait!" cried Connie. "I'll come with you."

He turned back for half a second, then strode on up the hill. "Suit yourself," he growled.

Connie returned from making a very brief explanation to Mrs. Haburn to find Maury so impatient she barely had the door closed before they were away like a streak of blue up the driveway.

After conferring with Billy Ray's foster family and with representatives from family and children services and the sheriff's office, Maury and Connie began their own search along the hilly Gainesville Road. They asked frequently at houses and businesses, but found no trace of a boy tall for his age, towheaded with, according to his foster mother, a five-dollar bill in his pocket. "I know he took it. It was change from when I bought gas," the woman said. "I put it on the refrigerator and now it's gone."

Gradually Maury's brittle edges began to smooth off a bit. "Sorry I was so raspy," he said to Connie as they drove along, scanning both sides of the highway. "It's not your fault he's missing. It's mine."

"Not just yours. It's circumstances. Billy Ray knew his parents had left. What a horrible rejection that was! Even if they were terrible, they were his parents, you know. His foster parents are good people, but they have five other children already. He'd been placed there in an emergency, and he knew he could be moved again any time. Maybe he'd begun to find some stability at school, but now it's ending up and the summer stretches ahead."

"You do have a way with words, Connie Jensen."

"And you are the one who matters most to Billy Ray, Maury."

"And I let him down, quit the church, and turned into a bear. Didn't I?"

Connie didn't answer. She searched the roadsides for any possible clue. Would someone be so irresponsible as to give a young boy a ride and not try to take him back where he belonged? The thought of the kinds of people who might pick him up for their own pleasures or gains made her shudder.

❧

Billy Ray walked all day Thursday and nearly all day Friday, but it was slow going since he had to stay out of sight all the time. A couple of times Friday he did get short rides. He wasn't afraid of much and certainly not of strangers. His own father would have scared him, but not strangers.

One of the strangers who gave him a lift was an elderly man on his way to the supermarket. Billy Ray told him he'd stayed home from school to take care of his

mother and she needed some ginger ale and some ant-
acid real, real bad. That ride saved him five miles of
trudging. The next one earned him a few more. Again,
he didn't ask for much. He didn't want this man smok-
ing a cigarette and looking sort of zonked to suspect his
story wasn't true. What he liked about that ride was the
dog in the back seat, a big, mean-looking German shep-
herd. He never growled at Billy Ray a single time and
the little boy took that as a good sign.

By nightfall Friday, he'd passed Alto and was very
glad. He didn't like being anywhere near that place where
big boys went to correctional school. They were the same
as in jail at that place. Pa had always yelled at him and
Lavon that they'd go there someday. Twenty more miles
to Gainesville, and his legs were so tired they could
hardly move anymore and blisters burned on both heels.
But he had to keep going, had to. He couldn't expect any
rides on this big road, especially at night.

He walked, scrambled, and slunk along the edges of
woods, high banks, and deep ditches. By now, he knew,
his foster mother would have reported to the school that
he wasn't sick at home. He'd bribed his foster brothers
and sister not to tell anything until they were asked. He'd
given one some cough drops, one a pair of pliers he'd
found by the road, one his only good shirt, but hardest of
all, he'd given away his sleek, silver harmonica. He'd
told Miss Jensen he wouldn't play anymore, that he'd
even buried it. But that wasn't true. He'd played every
private moment he'd had.

He wished he had his harmonica right now. He'd play
it to the stars and the moon. He put his hand in his jacket

pocket where his harmonica would have been and felt instead the five-dollar bill.

Smiling in the darkness he thought of breakfast. He would have breakfast in the morning. He finally got so tired he couldn't walk straight so he crawled into a culvert, curled an arm under his head, and, in fetal position, went sound asleep.

❧

Connie knew Maury was searching Friday every chance he could but, even after school, he didn't ask her to help him so she went on her own hunches. She didn't have any better success than she had on Thursday. Finally she went home and slept very poorly, rising before dawn to start toward Gainesville. If Billy Ray had made up his mind to go to the Gainesville airport in time for the eleven o'clock sky show, then somehow he would be there. And she would be, too.

When a semi full of empty chicken crates roared past her down below Alto, she had no idea that inside the cab a lonesome driver was listening with the greatest concern to a small boy's tale of his traumatic experience.

"Do you think my father's alive, mister? Can he still be alive?"

"Yes, yes. The fall out of the house didn't kill him instantly so he's probably going to be fine. Why was he working on his new house so early on Saturday morning?"

"Well, because something had to pass inspection or . . .I'm not sure. Mama didn't want him to. She cried and screamed at him, but he went anyway."

"And your mama followed?"

"Yes, sir. She put me and my baby sister in the car and lit out after him. Only by the time we got there, Daddy was lying—oh, it was awful! So she sent me to call an ambulance. Only a neighbor must have already called. When I got back they were leaving. In the ambulance. I yelled and waved my arms and ran after them, but it kept going and going."

"But you're sure it turned toward Gainesville? There's a good hospital in Habersham County, too."

"It went this way. I'm sure. Oh-h-h-h. I hope my daddy's all right." Real tears called on more tears and soon Billy Ray was shaking with sobs.

"Say, you know, you never told me your name," said the burly driver after a time.

"William Spencer," answered Billy Ray promptly, wiping his nose on a sleeve.

"Good name. Mine's Cliff Wheeler. Well, now, William Spencer, we're gonna be at that hospital in no time an' I'll go with you to the desk an' make sure they let you right in where your family is. Bet your mom's about frantic now worryin' about you. Good thing I'm ridin' empty so we can whiz up these hills."

"What do you carry in this thing?" asked Billy Ray, twisting in his seat belt.

"Chickens. Baby chicks to fill the chicken houses, broilers when they're ready for processing. Going to market, you know, so you can have that good ole fried chicken."

"I had a pet chicken once," said Billy Ray wistfully. His mind was working overtime. How would he shake this driver once they arrived at the hospital? He'd have to be fast, that was for sure. The blisters would just have to hurt. He couldn't believe how lucky he was to get a ride all the way to Gainesville. Now all he had to do, after getting away from this nice driver, was find the airport.

thirteen

As Connie parked at the airport early that Saturday morning, she remembered the first time she'd come here, how exciting it had been to see the parachutes coming down, especially that one with the red and white canopy. How happy Maury had been that day!

Pulling herself back to the present, she had to wonder if Billy Ray was anywhere in the vicinity. Maybe he *had* gone searching for his family. No one knew yet. But she had a feeling, a strong feeling, that Billy Ray would be at the airport soon.

She spied a telephone booth and hurried toward it. Just maybe Maury might know something by now. Of course he probably was anywhere but at home. He'd either be searching for Billy Ray or getting ready to fly.

As she waited for an answer, she scanned the skies from the phone booth. Clear and gorgeous. The sun's rays brushed pink on the horizon. It would be a wonderful day for Maury to parachute. But if they couldn't find Billy Ray, he wouldn't enjoy it at all.

A female voice answered huskily. Connie was confused. Had she dialed the wrong number? Was Maury's mother with him? Not on a flying day! She hung up and left the phone booth as if a bee had bitten her.

She sat in her car, oblivious now to the sunrise, the drift of a windsock, or to early morning walkers using a runway for their track. She hugged herself against a chill and realized her teeth were chattering. It was end of May, not that cold.

Now she understood clearly why Maury hadn't asked her to help him hunt for Billy Ray yesterday. He'd already had plans before Billy Ray complicated things. No wonder he'd been so indifferent whenever she mentioned his doing something with Billy Ray the last few weeks. All the time she thought he was still mourning his friend and trying to make sense out of his life. And of course he didn't want to get serious about her. Oh, no! Because he had someone else all the time. How could she have been so. . .naive!

And what to do now? To leave was most appealing. But there was still Billy Ray. Maury wasn't hunting for him, so she had to. She must stick to her post. That's all she had to worry about right now. Stick to the airport like a veritable private eye until she saw that little blond-headed boy.

Nine and nine-thirty came and went. People were beginning to arrive for the show. Connie recognized a few faces and felt a pang of her own grief for Jock and Betty, who should have been there. Seconds ticked away. Where was Maury? Aside from everything else, Maury was a faithful person. He wouldn't willfully let his team or anyone down once he'd made a promise. He just didn't make promises very readily. And where, oh where was Billy Ray?

Raising Jean's binoculars one more time, Connie scanned the whole airport and was about to lay them down with a sigh when a gasp escaped her instead. *There* he was! Billy Ray. Getting out of a blue pickup truck. Maury's! Maury ran inside the building, leaving Billy Ray behind, but not alone. Who was that with Billy Ray? It wasn't his foster mother, certainly not his mother. Short curly blond hair, bright pink cheeks, arm across Billy Ray's shoulders. They disappeared inside the building. The voice she'd heard on the phone, she was sure, went with that curly blond hair. Connie fought nausea.

❧

"You should have stayed to see what all happened, dearie," soothed Mrs. Haburn, later that day as she poured Connie a bracing cup of tea. "You know, you owe that much to Maury Donovan. You shoulda let him explain."

"I don't guess I owe him very much. He cut the strings, if there were any, pretty thoroughly. Only I just wouldn't let go. In my mind I was still hoping. I know that now. I couldn't confront them down there, Mrs. Haburn. As long as Billy Ray was okay, I thought I should leave. Anyway, to tell the truth, I didn't really think much. I was so stunned, so. . .overwhelmed. . .I couldn't."

"Tell me again what she looked like."

"Oh, Mrs. Haburn, she was beautiful! Curly blond hair, a gorgeous figure."

"Could be a lot of folks, includin' Dolly Parton and Barbara Mandrell," said Mrs. Haburn, setting some cream down for the cat.

"Oh, don't try to make me laugh. This isn't funny!"

"Sorry, honey, I know it ain't. Just hate to see you so sad."

The phone rang and both women looked at it hanging

there on the wall like a living, breathing intruder. At the third ring Mrs. Haburn answered it. Her face lit up.

"Oh, hi, Billy Ray. I've heard a lot about you. Yes, sure you can speak to Miss Jensen. Right here she is."

When Connie hung up, her eyes were dull. "He's okay so I should be glad. It was time for Maury's plane to go up so he told Billy Ray to call me. Maury had called earlier and I wasn't here yet. You must have been outside."

Mrs. Haburn nodded. "Went down to check on the blueberries."

Connie sat back down. "He said Miss Tatum was real nice and would let him stay at her place tonight because his foster mother already said she doesn't want him back. I'm not sure how he knew that, but I don't guess it matters. Anyway, he wasn't worried at all, just kind of breathless with excitement, getting ready to go watch the sky show. At least *his* dream is coming true."

"Oh, dear, I think this calls for another cup of tea," said Mrs. Haburn, gathering Connie's cup.

"No. No, thanks, Mrs. Haburn. I've had enough tea. I need something else. I'm going for a walk."

"You should have learned how to fish. That's the best unkinking thing to do," said Mrs. Haburn, who was rewarded by Connie's watery smile.

❧

Connie watched the ducks for a few minutes, but they were becoming very snobbish and discourteous since she hadn't brought them any crumbs. She walked between rows of blueberry bushes and paused to lift one branch, heavy with green berries. Something soft pushed gently against her leg and she bent to scoop up the yellow cat. "Left your cream to come comfort me, did you?" she asked, laying her cheek against the silken fur.

High up on the hill, she looked back east across the pond to where slopes of forest beyond the road basked in afternoon sun like green furry monsters cuddled up to sleep. Shadows darkened the dips and crevices of shoulders, haunches, and paws. Nearby, the pond lay motionless, mirroring a scene so much bigger than itself. A thrush sang somewhere behind her. The song that usually made her so happy, now brought tears to her eyes.

"I've really been pretty useless lately, Lord, what with worrying about my own situation so much. But I know You're not through with me yet, and I'm depending on You to make something out of this mess. I don't even know what to pray for except. . .please be with me."

Shadows lengthened. A stiff breeze rippled the pond, zigzagging its reflections of trees and sky. More birds, inspired by the thrush, began to sing. Connie became aware of a spicy sweet scent carried lightly on the wind.

She would not think about Maury's exuberance after his jump and of someone else being there to catch the light of his joy. She would not think about Billy Ray happily skipping between the two of them. She would not think.

"Thanks, Lord, for bringing Billy Ray back and for taking care of him. Help him day by day to replace his hate with love. He's such a sweet little fellow underneath his cover. I hope. . . .Send him a good teacher next year, please, someone who will believe in him. And give him a permanent home with security. I don't ask much, do I?"

She picked up a stick and tossed it where the cat was stalking, so startling the poor creature that he forgot his real prey and pounced on the stick instead, rolling over with it in his briery grasp.

"And, Lord, please take care of Maury Donovan," said Connie as she rose to follow her well-worn trail back down the hill.

fourteen

Connie had been back home in Augusta for two weeks. Those last few days at Pine Ridge after the children were out seemed nothing but an unhappy blur. Maury had been courteous, even kind when she had to talk to him professionally, but that was all. What little she learned about Billy Ray's being found was from Zena, who said the child was now staying temporarily with his caseworker.

When she got her first letter from Mrs. Haburn, she scanned it quickly for any mention of Maury Donovan. Even the smallest bit of news would be wonderful. But she didn't see his name anywhere. Billy Ray's name filled up the whole letter. What did Mrs. Haburn have to say about Billy Ray? But wait—what was this clipping? The announcement of a Miss Candace Tatum's upcoming marriage? Miss Tatum? She looked at the smiling picture and wanted to tear it to very shreds then and there. Though she'd only seen the woman through binoculars that day, she was sure this was the same person. And Maury was marrying her? How *could* he after telling her. . .what had he told her? Was this the same man who couldn't get serious?

With a mixture of reluctance and insatiable curiosity, Connie began to read the wedding announcement and cried out in amazement. The groom's name was Edward Clark. A man's name had never looked so wonderful!

She kissed the piece of paper that moments earlier she'd wanted to shred.

But back to the letter. What was this about Billy Ray?

"After you left," wrote Mrs. Haburn in a jerky kind of handwriting that sort of wandered downhill, "I was too lonesome. Not enough to do. I knew that little boy needed a place. And lots of love. I've got both. So I called that family services place. That Miss Tatum is the one I got. You'll remember her when you see her picture. She's Billy Ray's caseworker. A real nice person.

"Anyways, Billy Ray's living with me now, staying in your room. He's not near quiet like you, but he can sure catch a fish! He's almost as picky as you about anybody prying into his affairs, but I keep prying anyways. I'm not afraid of him at all, 'cause I just don't live that way. I may be a mite foolish, maybe a whole lot foolish, but I do want to do this."

Connie bit her lip. Miss Tatum was Billy Ray's caseworker. That explained some things. Her cheeks warmed at the very thought of how easily she'd jumped to conclusions. On the other hand, she still didn't quite see why the woman was at Maury's house answering his phone at 6:30 in the morning. She read the letter over, amazed again at Mrs. Haburn's generosity and energy. What a wonderful place for Billy Ray if Mrs. Haburn could manage it. Billy Ray could outrun her coming and going, but if anyone could outwit him, it was Mrs. Haburn.

The next time she heard from Mrs. Haburn, her letter went on and on about how many blueberries she and Billy Ray had picked, how many picking customers they'd had, how fast a picker Billy Ray was, how many pints she'd frozen, how many canned, and how much jam she'd made. Connie was surprised there weren't blueberry stains all over the paper since she could easily picture Mrs.Haburn hunched over her letter writing at the same table with buckets of blueberries.

But Mrs. Haburn had poured out her very best news at the bottom of the last page: In a different color of ink, words scrambled to the bottom of the page and climbed back up the sides. The handwriting was more atrocious than ever, written in such excitement.

"Glad I didn't mail this yesterday. Would have to start up a whole new letter if I had. Your prayers and mine are done answered, Connie! We knowed that fine Maury Donovan weren't happy being a principal. Well, listen to this. Reverend Stone preached a sermon today that made everyone want to give whatever they had to the Lord, even if they went to the poorhouse. And what some has to give is more than money.

"Mr. Maury Donovan was there. He's been coming to pick me and Billy Ray up for church ever since you left. Well, I could tell Maury was awful fidgety. I thought maybe he was in a hurry or had a stomachache or at least a bad case of chiggers. But when Phil gave the invitation, guess who was the first one down that aisle? Maury Donovan! He talked to the church, told us he was sorry he'd been so wishy-washy and that he knew now that God wanted him to be a minister of music, that he'd tried to get out of it long enough. Get this. He's going to seminary in September!"

Connie burst out into excited screams. It was unbelievable! Yet it was true. She grabbed her sunglasses from the hall table and went jogging. She simply could not stay in the house knowing such big news; she had to get outside and be doing something. If only her mother were home, someone to rejoice with her.

When Connie got back from running two miles, she read the letter again and again, smiling at Mrs. Haburn's closing that was scrawled along the side of the page: "Now I've run clean out of paper. You take care, honey. Love and prayers. Hilda Haburn."

She'd write Mrs. Haburn back right now, that's what she'd do. Or should she call? She'd do both!

❧

She wondered if maybe Maury would call her, now that so much was changed. But weeks went by and the only news she received was from Mrs. Haburn and Jean. Maury would be moving to Louisville, Kentucky. He was working with their church until he left sometime in August. Also he was working at the school, getting it in tiptop shape for the new principal who, at last report, hadn't been found.

Could she call him? Not when he'd made it so abundantly clear he didn't want to get involved with her. Yet some of his reasons had been removed, hadn't they? Maybe not *his* reasons. No, she couldn't call, no matter how much she wanted to.

It was a hot sizzling day late in July when Mrs. Jensen called Connie to the phone. A familiar deep voice said, "Hi! Connie? Maury here. I need to see you." Just like him not to beat around the bush.

She took a deep breath. "When?"

"Ten minutes? I'm at the airport. Flew down with one of the guys. We're jumping this afternoon."

"Give me thirty minutes. I'll meet you at the airport."

Ten minutes indeed! The crazy man! No word in all this time, then suddenly, "Meet me in ten minutes!" She smiled to herself. She was going, wasn't she? But not before she changed from shorts to an ankle-length gauzy blue skirt and white tee shirt. Fastening her favorite gold earrings in place and giving her dark hair a brisk brushing, she dashed out the door.

&

He was bigger than ever and his eyes bluer. He'd even grown a beard, a neatly trimmed one. He was gorgeous. She smiled uncertainly as she started toward him, but his face lit up when he saw her and he leaped to his feet, covering the distance between them in three big strides.

"Connie! Oh, you look so. . .very wonderful!"

"Thanks very much," she said stiffly, putting out a hand.

His smile faded and dark brows knit together. "We need to talk and this place is too noisy."

"Come on," said Connie. "I'll take you for a ride."

"No. Let's just walk outside. Our jump is in another hour or so. I need to stay close. Anyway, I want you to listen to me, not drive."

"You're still jumping then?"

"Yes. This will be the last one for a long time. I'm going to be a student again—"

"Mrs. Haburn told me the wonderful news. Maury, I'm so glad! I can tell you're happy. Your face is so much more relaxed, at peace. What I can see of it," she ended on a tease.

He rubbed a hand across his bristly jaw and grinned.

They walked around the end of the building where they could see several small planes tied down. The sky above was clear blue, and the windsock was barely moving.

"Augusta is always like this in July," Connie said. "Humidity and mosquitoes thick enough to butcher for supper, my daddy always says. You can see why in the old days everyone who could hopped on a train and went to the north Georgia mountains."

"Augusta has its calling cards, too," said Maury, grinning down at her.

"Tell me what happened, Maury."

He drew a deep breath, then slowly exhaled, hands deep in the pockets of his light khakis. "It still seems too big to confine to mere words," he said. "When I finally let go and told God He could have all of me—school, flying, you, everything—He put the pieces in place for me. I'm on His timetable now. It's like I've been released from a ten-year confinement. I've lost a lot of time worrying about what couldn't be helped. . .like my father's death. But God's taking it from here."

"Your mother?" asked Connie.

He sighed. "She doesn't like my going into the music ministry and was bitterly opposed to my giving up the principal's job. Maybe someday she'll accept it all. I hope so."

They'd gone around the building now. Maury stopped at a corner and leaned against the wall. "Connie, I don't think I've a right to say anything to you, but I. . .well, I know you misunderstood some things."

"Such as?" The pain had returned and it made her harden her chin, straighten her back.

"Well, Mrs. Haburn says you called my house early in the morning that day—"

"Yes and a young woman answered the phone. I remember the sun was just coming up."

"Miss Tatum. She's Billy Ray's caseworker. She was hunting for Billy Ray the day before, and I knew it, though we hadn't been together." He saw her disbelief, but shoved on. "She'd given me her number in case I heard anything. We did not spend the night together, Connie!"

"So what happened?" she asked.

"I'd called all the area hospitals and told them to report to me anything to do with an eight-year-old blond boy's injury. Well, they called that morning from Gainesville's hospital and told me this weird story about a chicken truck driver who'd brought a boy in to see his parents, only the parents weren't there and the boy had disappeared while the truck driver was inquiring. I knew it had to be Billy Ray. Doesn't it sound just like him?"

For the first time they smiled together, mutually enjoying the scene they could both so easily picture.

"Well, I called Miss Tatum right quick as I'd promised to do, and she said she'd be right there. She must have been up and dressed already. She came so quickly I was still pulling my socks on. Right after she got there, the phone rang. I nodded for her to please answer it because she was nearer and I assumed the call would be about Billy Ray anyway. I guess that was you."

"It was."

"Connie, I'm sorry. I didn't even know for a long time

that that was you or think of how it looked to you."

"You didn't know I went to the airport, too?"

"Not till recently."

"How did you find Billy Ray?"

"Looked everywhere between that hospital and the airport and finally spied him sitting on a curb looking totally tuckered out. You should have seen him when I pulled up beside him!"

"I would have liked that."

"Connie, there was never anything between me and Miss Tatum, never. It was so far from my mind, I was staggered when Mrs. Haburn showed me how it looked to you."

"Does it really make any difference now?" she asked.

"I hope so," he said, putting a finger under her chin to make her look at him. "I hope you can forgive me for all the times I hurt you. I want your forgiveness, Connie."

"You have it, Maury. Really."

"But that's not all I want." He hadn't moved his hand.

"What else?"

Heat waves shimmered a foot above the asphalt. A light plane touched down and coasted to a halt. But for Connie the world had stopped. She wanted to believe what she saw in Maury's eyes, that hungry, wistful look. That look that made her feel like the most desirable woman in the world. But was all this real or was she dreaming?

Slowly Maury placed hands on her shoulders, then framed her face with them.

"I'm so completely in love with you, I've been missing you every minute you've been gone and kicking myself for making such stupid mistakes. My only defense is, God hadn't knocked sense into me yet."

His face was only inches away now. His eyes were filled with warm light that made the blue sparkle like sunny lakes. His lips touched hers very, very gently like a plea. Then, finding her submissive, he kissed her again, and she nestled against him with a sigh that was almost a sob.

"This is what I came for," he said.

"Silly. You came to jump, remember?"

"No. That was just my excuse. You know what this means?" he asked against her hair.

"No. What does it mean?"

"It means I'm very, very serious about you. And I hope you can be serious about me."

She laughed softly. "Serious?"

"Serious. As in, will you marry me?"

She pulled away from him, the better to study his face. "Maury? Are you sure you want such a burden?"

He laughed. "I not only want you, I need you, burdens and all. I love you, Connie."

"I love you, too, with all my heart. Yes. Yes! I'll marry you." Impulsively, she stood on tiptoes and kissed him.

Behind them someone noisily cleared his throat. "Maury! Time to suit up!"

Maury cupped Connie's chin in one hand. Her eyes now were alive with dancing lights. "I won't go if you really don't want me to. I'm willing to stop jumping right now if that's what it takes to win you."

"It was never my idea for you to stop sky diving, remember? I'll be waiting when you come down. Now, you better run!"

There were several jumpers, but they weren't prepared to make formations, only to come down singly. Connie wished she had Jean's binoculars and vowed she'd get some of her own. It was quite a while after the jumpers were out before Connie could be sure which one was Maury, but as soon as she did, she began trying to figure out just where he'd stand down so she could be nearby.

He was almost down when she heard his big voice singing in the sky, belting out an ecstatic melody for all to hear: "Then sings my soul, my Saviour God to thee, how great Thou art, how great Thou art!"

"He's coming down 'On Wings of Song,' " she whispered, knowing without a doubt she'd follow him wherever the Lord sent him.

A Letter To Our Readers

Dear Reader:

In order that we might better contribute to your reading enjoyment, we would appreciate your taking a few minutes to respond to the following questions. When completed, please return to the following:

Rebecca Germany, Editor
Heartsong Presents
P.O. Box 719
Uhrichsville, Ohio 44683

1. Did you enjoy reading *On Wings of Song*?
   - ❏ Very much. I would like to see more books by this author!
   - ❏ Moderately
     I would have enjoyed it more if _____

   _____

2. Are you a member of **Heartsong Presents**? ❏ Yes ❏ No
   If no, where did you purchase this book?_____

   _____

3. What influenced your decision to purchase this book? (Check those that apply.)

❏ Cover	❏ Back cover copy
❏ Title	❏ Friends
❏ Publicity	❏ Other_____

4. How would you rate, on a scale from 1 (poor) to 5 (superior), the cover design? _____

5. On a scale from 1 (poor) to 10 (superior), please rate the following elements.

    ___Heroine   ___Plot

    ___Hero   ___ Inspirational theme

    ___Setting   ___Secondary characters

6. What settings would you like to see covered in **Heartsong Presents** books?_____

_____

_____

7. What are some inspirational themes you would like to see treated in future books?_____

_____

_____

8. Would you be interested in reading other **Heartsong Presents** titles?   ❑ Yes   ❑ No

9. Please check your age range:
   ❑ Under 18   ❑ 18-24   ❑ 25-34
   ❑ 35-45   ❑ 46-55   ❑ Over 55

10. How many hours per week do you read? _____

Name _____

Occupation _____

Address _____

City_____ State_____ Zip_____

Introducing New Authors!

___ **Nancy Lavo**—*A Change of Heart*—When Laura Wells's father is unable to accompany her on a much anticipated Caribbean cruise, Graham Kirkland agrees to chaperon Laura and her bubbly friend, Kathi. Turbulent waters are ahead as Laura must learn to release her anger toward God. HP133 $2.95

___ **Phyllis A. Humphrey**—*Flying High*—When Kelly Marsh's job forces her into contact with Steven Barry, the dark, arrogant skydiver, Kelly is immediately skeptical. Kelly can't have fallen in love with Steven, a non-Christian with such a dangerous and frivolous career. Yet, when God touches the most stubborn hearts, miracles can happen. HP142 $2.95

___ **Peggy Darty**—*Morning Mountain*—Suzanne is confident she'll find a way to keep the family ranch, but she is unprepared to handle the wounded stranger she finds in the hills. His mysterious ways, the wedding ring in his bag, and the way he comes and goes like a shadow can only bring trouble. HP143 $2.95

___ **Cara McCormack**—*Drewry's Bluff*—When Drewry's uncle promises her in marriage in payment of a gambling debt, she feels she must take matters into her own hands, and quickly! Through an unexpected turn of events, she arrives in Richmond, ready to assume a new identity as nanny to the two young children of wealthy plantation owner and widower Chase Auburn. HP147 $2.95

Send to: **Heartsong Presents** Reader's Service
P.O. Box 719
Uhrichsville, Ohio 44683

Please send me the items checked above. I am enclosing
$_____(please add $1.00 to cover postage and handling per order. OH add 6.25% tax. NJ add 6% tax.)
Send check or money order, no cash or C.O.D.s, please.
To place a credit card order, call 1-800-847-8270.

NAME _____

ADDRESS _____

CITY/STATE _____ ZIP _____

NEW4

······ Presents ······

Great Inspirational Romance at a Great Price!

Heartsong Presents books are inspirational romances in contemporary and historical settings, designed to give you an enjoyable, spirit-lifting reading experience. You can choose from 160 wonderfully written titles from some of today's best authors like Veda Boyd Jones, Yvonne Lehman, Tracie J. Peterson, and many others.

When ordering quantities less than twelve, above titles are $2.95 each.

SEND TO: Heartsong Presents Reader's Service
P.O. Box 719, Uhrichsville, Ohio 44683

Please send me the items checked above. I am enclosing $_____
(please add $1.00 to cover postage per order. OH add 6.25% tax. NJ
add 6%.). Send check or money order, no cash or C.O.D.s, please.
To place a credit card order, call 1-800-847-8270.

NAME _____

ADDRESS _____

CITY/STATE_____ ZIP _____

HPS 1-96